THE PREGNANT PROPOSITION

BY
SANDRA PAUL

MILLS & BOON

All the characters in this book have no existence outside the imagination of the author, and have no relation whatsoever to anyone bearing the same name or names. They are not even distantly inspired by any individual known or unknown to the author, and all the incidents are pure invention.

First published in Great Britain 2011
Harlequin Mills & Boon Limited,
Eton House, 18-24 Paradise Road, Richmond, Surrey TW9 1SR

THE PREGNANT PROPOSITION © Sandra Novy Chvostal 2010

ISBN: 978 0 263 88865 2

23-0211

Harlequin Mills & Boon policy is to use papers that are natural, renewable and recyclable products and made from wood grown in sustainable forests. The logging and manufacturing processes conform to the legal environmental regulations of the country of origin.

Printed and bound in Spain
by Litografia Rosés S.A., Barcelona

Sandra Paul married her high school sweetheart and they live in Southern California. They have three children, three cats, and one overgrown "puppy."

Sandra has a degree in journalism, but prefers to write from the heart. When she isn't busy working as a Housekeeper, Gardener, Animal Trainer, Short Order Cook, Accountant, Caregiver, Interior Designer, Nutritional Researcher, Chauffeur, Hotline Love Advisor, Handywoman, Landscape Architect, Business Consultant, or serving as the primary volunteer for the Rocking Horse Rescue, she loves to create stories that end in happily ever after.

Dedicated with love to
Leonard Novy
Thelma (Novy) Weyher
Norma (Novy) Benish
and Virgil Frank Novy.
We miss you all so much.

Chapter One

"The first step in initiating a successful breeding program is taking the time to observe the available animals. Begin by evaluating temperament as well as physical soundness, or the lack thereof…"
—*Successful Breeding: A Guide for the Cattleman*

From the top of the hill, Allyson Cabrerra caught sight of the black pickup as it pulled off the shimmering highway onto the graveled patch that served the old cemetery for parking. Brand-spanking-new and disgustingly expensive, the tricked-out diesel was the kind that, in the tiny town of Tangleweed, only an O'Malley would own.

Sure enough, the dust hadn't settled around the truck's shiny chrome hubcaps before Troy Michael O'Malley climbed out.

Ally stiffened—the involuntary reaction of all Cabrerras whenever they spotted an O'Malley—and glanced across the gleaming black casket at her four older brothers. None had noticed Troy yet. All stood with their backs to the road and boots firmly planted on the coarse buffalo grass that littered the hillside. Hats clasped in their work-roughened hands, their dark heads were bowed beneath the searing west Texas sun as they listened to Reverend Smith pray for their late maternal great-aunt, Eileen Hennessey.

"Hear us, oh Lord, in our time of sorrow and grief...."

Neither Sue Ellen Pickart nor Emma Mae Downs, contemporaries of Ally's late great-aunt, noticed Troy, either. Sue Ellen—who enjoyed funerals almost as much as her daily soaps—had her plump face buried in a crumpled pink tissue and was sobbing so noisily even the Reverend's deep baritone could barely be heard above her wailing. While Emma—there to cover the "event" for the *Tangleweed Times*—stood with wrinkled cheeks sucked in and eyes tightly closed as she concentrated on punctuating each of the Reverend's utterances with a hearty "amen."

Next to Emma, Janie Smith, the Reverend's daughter, faithfully echoed the older women's outbursts in a faint, breathless voice. Her pale cheeks reddened from the heat and painful shyness, Janie kept her eyes fixed on the toes of her flat-heeled shoes, obviously trying to avoid drawing the attention of any of those "alarming" Cabrerra brothers.

No one else had bothered to attend the funeral. The Cabrerra siblings weren't especially social—discounting the brothers' interactions with the single women in the county—and during the last twenty of her eighty-some years, Aunt Eileen had been a virtual hermit. So only Ally saw Troy stand by his truck looking toward the small funeral party before he retrieved a bunch of yellow flowers from the cab.

Then, slamming the door shut, he headed toward the cemetery gate.

Ally tried to ignore him, to concentrate on her feelings for her late great-aunt, but her emotions were regretfully vague. The sad truth was, Aunt Eileen had always kept an emotional distance from everyone when alive, and death hadn't brought her any closer. Troy, on the other hand, was moving much closer. From the corner of her eye, Ally watched him as the Reverend droned on.

"Yea, though I walk through the valley of the shadow of death…"

"Amen!" declared Emma.

"Amen," whispered Janie.

"Boo-hoo!" sobbed Sue Ellen, sniffing.

"I will fear no evil…."

Ally "amened" absently with the other women as the Reverend paused, but her attention remained on Troy. She didn't fear him, of course—but only a fool took their eyes off a moving snake. This snake, she noted, had a hitch in his step, most likely a legacy from the awkward way he'd fallen when bull riding at the rodeo last Saturday, after beating out her second oldest brother Kyle by six points.

"In the presence of my enemies…"

"Amen!"

"Amen."

"Boo-hoo!"

"I will trust in the Lord…."

You certainly couldn't trust an O'Malley, Ally reflected, unless maybe you were one. Troy and his grandfather Mick were pretty tight; she'd give them that much. And although Troy's second cousins had all moved out of state, they flocked back to the O'Malley homestead every Christmas, as faithful as geese migrating to a favorite pond.

Troy must have come to place flowers on his family's plot, Ally decided, as he strode toward well-tended grave sites surrounded by a wrought-iron railing. Like the Cabrerras, generations of O'Malleys were buried up and down the hillside, including Troy's parents. But when Troy didn't even pause to glance at the elaborate headstone on his parents' grave—located a bare ten feet from the more modest one that marked her own parents'—Ally tensed again.

He can't be coming here, she thought, as he continued through the maze of older grave sites that bordered the cemetery. Troy might be arrogant, but she'd never thought he was stupid.

Apparently, she'd overestimated his mental abilities, because Troy kept walking.

"Who shall ascend onto the hill of the Lord?" the Reverend demanded, gazing at his Bible as Troy started up the worn path toward the funeral party. "Who shall stand in his holy place?"

Not Troy, Ally decided, eying his steady approach. Or at least he wouldn't be standing long once her brothers caught sight of him. If Kyle didn't throw him back down the hillside, then the twins surely would. Lincoln and Luke were still pissed off about a fight they'd gotten into with Troy a couple of weeks ago in Big Bob's Bar and Grill, resulting in a decree by the local sheriff—heartily upheld by Big Bob—forbidding the twins to return for at least a month.

"Only he that hath clean hands, and a pure heart can enter the Lord's domain…." the Reverend declared.

A pure heart? That was something an O'Malley could never claim. Just look at how Troy's grandfather had treated poor Aunt Eileen. And what had happened between Troy and Misty Sanderson.

"Who hath not lifted his soul unto vanity, nor sworn deceitfully…"

All the O'Malleys were deceitful, from old Mick on down;

Ally had learned *that* in her cradle. As for vanity—please! Troy O'Malley was so vain she was surprised he didn't carry a full-length mirror. Yeah, he knew how attractive he was—to women whose intelligence quotient was equal to their bust size, anyway. At the Houston Rodeo last spring Ally had actually seen a woman trip over her own pink, pedicured toes and fall facedown into the sawdust when Troy threw a wicked, green-eyed glance her way.

"He shall receive blessings from the Lord…."

And not only had Troy been blessed with good looks, he'd been blessed with the money to play them up, as well. When bull riding he wore the usual cowboy outfit of Western shirt and Wranglers, but today he was dressed, as Aunt Eileen would have said, fit for a funeral or Sunday dinner. His charcoal-gray suit made his broad build look leaner and taller. His white shirt was crisp, his hand-tooled boots polished. He made Ally conscious suddenly that none of her brothers, in their well-worn jackets, looked half so slick. That beneath her wide-brimmed straw hat her dark hair needed cutting and her navy-blue dress—bought for her high school graduation six years earlier—had never been very becoming to begin with.

Her eyes narrowed on Troy's tanned face, which was shadowed by his expensive gray Stetson, as he reached the top of the rocky path. A hot flush of resentment swept over her. It wasn't a person's clothes that were important, but what kind of person they were, she told herself. Still, she wished she'd taken more time with her appearance. Because apparently not content with the ill will that already existed between their families, for the past year Troy had elevated the conflict to a more personal level—needling Ally every chance he got. And, oh, how she hated supplying him with ammunition.

Irritably, she swatted at a gnat hovering by her cheek, and at her movement, Troy looked up. Their gazes locked. For a second he remained inscrutable as his green eyes flickered over her face. Then he smiled, his expression shifting to the slightly mocking look Ally knew all too well.

She scowled in return, and Troy's smile broadened. Ally must have made a disgusted sound, because Janie glanced at her questioningly, then followed her gaze as the Reverend concluded.

"Amen!" intoned Emma Mae.

"A-man! I mean, amen!" gasped Janie, her hand flying up to cover her mouth.

"Boo— Ooooooh!" wheezed Sue Ellen, her plump face brightening as she, too, caught sight of Troy.

Kyle's head had jerked up at Janie's gasp. He turned—stiffening at the sight of an O'Malley approaching. Without removing his gaze from Troy, Kyle elbowed Linc hard in the ribs. Linc stumbled against Luke, who slipped on the rocky hillside, his arms flailing briefly before he regained his balance.

Ally winced, amazed as always that her leggy brother could be so graceful in the saddle, and so awkward standing on his own two feet. But Luke's clumsiness was forgotten as she caught sight of her oldest brother's face as he, too, glanced back at Troy. Although all the Cabrerras had their Latino father's black hair and golden skin, they'd inherited their Irish mother's eyes—a dark true blue. But in the harsh sunlight, Cole's narrowed gaze looked like slits of frozen blue ice.

For once, the Reverend appeared speechless. Silence fell on the small group, broken only by the sound of cicadas buzzing in the bushes and Sue Ellen's wheezy breathing.

"What are you doing here, O'Malley?" Cole finally demanded.

"Paying my final respects to Miss Hennessey," Troy replied, moving forward toward Ally, so close his broad shadow enveloped her smaller one on the dusty ground. When he removed his hat, his arm brushed hers and she edged away. He glanced down at her, adding with an exaggerated drawl in his voice, "I considered her a friend of mine."

His challenging gaze lifted again to sweep the small party. Cole's face hardened even more and Kyle and the twins shifted restlessly. Ally could almost feel the tension rising in the hot still air as the men eyed one another without blinking. The Reverend must have felt it, too, because he suddenly cleared his throat. His deep voice was extra-hearty as he declared, "Welcome, Troy, welcome. Now, let us all join together in reciting the Lord's Prayer."

Emma led the way, followed dutifully by Janie and absently by Sue Ellen, who'd forgotten to sob and was quivering with excitement as her avid gaze darted between Cole and Troy, reminding Ally irresistibly of Emma's plump poodle eying a gourmet treat. Ally prayed along, too, and one by one the men added their voices to the mix.

They made it through the rest of the short service without incident. No one said a word, not even when Troy laid yellow roses—Aunt Eileen's favorites—on the casket, their heavy, sweet perfume thickening the hot air and drawing the gnats their way. It wasn't until the group had made its way down the hill that tempers flared once again.

Troy started it, of course. The O'Malleys were always starting trouble. Troy stood silent as Cole, pointedly ignoring Troy, invited the rest of the funeral party to the ranch house. But when Ally turned to follow the small group heading toward their cars, Troy caught her by the elbow to stop her.

His grasp was light, but his long fingers radiated heat, making her skin prickle beneath her sleeve. Pulling away from his grip, she shot him a suspicious look.

He stared down at her, his expression solemn for once. "My sympathy for your loss."

"Thank you," she responded warily.

Her cautious tone made the corners of his eyes crinkle slightly with amusement, but his tone remained serious as he said, "This isn't the time or place to do business, but I'd like to meet with you this week. To discuss Bride's Price."

Before Ally could respond, Cole—who'd turned back to see what was going on—reached her side. "There's nothing to discuss, O'Malley," Cole stated as the rest of the party rejoined them. Taking her other arm, Cole tugged Ally farther from Troy, adding, "I told you Bride's Price isn't for sale."

Troy met Cole's stare with narrowed eyes. "Yeah, you told me that. What you didn't tell me was that your sister's the one Miss Hennessey left the land to." His gaze caught Ally's. "Didn't she?"

She nodded and Cole spoke up again. "Ally owns the land," he conceded, "but my aunt put it in a trust to be controlled by me until Al turns thirty or marries." His voice dropped to a harsh, taunting tone. "She's only twenty-four, O'Malley. Why don't you come back in six years?"

Cole didn't add "or when she gets married," Ally noticed. Clearly her brother didn't even consider that a possibility. Her glance swept the rest of the faces intently watching the exchange. Nor, she realized wryly, did anyone else.

Including Troy O'Malley. Eyes narrowing, he frowned at her brother, then bit out, "All right, if you won't sell, then I'll lease Bride's Price from you." He named a sum that made Cole's dark eyebrows lift involuntarily in surprise and Ally's heart leap with excitement. With that kind of money, she could—

"Sorry," Cole said, interrupting Ally's thoughts. He didn't look sorry, however, but grimly satisfied as he added, "But the answer's still no."

A muscle flexed in Troy's square jaw. "That parcel is O'Malley land. You know it and I know it. Now that Eileen's gone, it's time to return it to its rightful owners."

"All I know is that your grandfather deeded that land to my great-aunt and it now belongs to our family," Cole said.

"He only gave it to her because they were betrothed."

"He gave it to her as a gift," Ally corrected Troy before Cole could reply. "There were no strings attached."

Troy spared her an impatient glance. "He was expecting to marry her."

"I see," Ally said thoughtfully. "So Mick was actually giving himself a gift. How like an O'Malley," she drawled, and watched Troy's scowl darken. Pleased by the sight, she added, "Rather stupid of him to cheat on her, then, wasn't it?"

This time the look Troy returned was longer. "Men often do stupid things when it comes to women."

"I certainly won't argue with an expert on that," Ally answered.

One of the twins snickered, while Sue Ellen gasped excitedly. Emma clucked her tongue.

But Troy merely stared at her a moment longer, silently promising future retribution, before his gaze shifted to Cole. He gave a shrug. "What's past is past. It doesn't have any bearing on my offer to either buy or lease that land—offers you'd be wise to rethink, Cabrerra."

"Oh, yeah?" Cole drawled, widening his stance and placing his hands on his hips. "Why's that?"

"Because from what I hear you've spread yourself thin lately, financially speaking, and can use the money."

Cole didn't like that; Ally could tell by the way his voice grew soft. "Where'd you hear that?"

"From a mutual friend," Troy drawled, his tone just as soft and even more taunting than Cole's had been.

The mutual friend, Ally knew, had to be Misty. Apparently her oldest brother knew it, too, because for a second, sheer hatred burned in Cole's icy eyes. He took a step in Troy's direction. Troy stepped forward to meet him, and funeral or no funeral, there would have been a fight—Ally was sure of it—but the Reverend grasped Cole's arm, holding him off.

Cole didn't resist the Reverend, but he didn't look away from Troy's steady gaze, either. "Later, O'Malley."

Troy nodded. "Yeah, later." With a final, mocking look at Ally, and a polite tilt of his hat to the other women, he headed toward the parking area.

The other men slowly followed, while the women stood in silence, watching until Troy climbed into his pickup.

"Well, thank goodness that's over, and without violence, too," Sue Ellen said, disappointment heavy in her quavery voice as Troy's truck spewed gravel pulling out of the tiny lot, and sped to the highway with small tornadoes of dust churning behind its oversize tires. She heaved a sigh, then patted Ally's arm as they started walking toward the cars again. "You are so lucky, dear, to have four brothers to watch out for you!"

"You certainly are!" Emma stated.

Ally wasn't sure she agreed. She planned to talk to Cole as soon as possible concerning the decisions he'd made—without consulting her, thank you very much!—about Bride's Price. But for the next two hours she was too busy playing hostess, serving up the tuna-and-pea casserole Emma Mae had brought and making sure everyone had plenty of coffee and second helpings of Sue Ellen's famous peach cobbler, to even try to catch Cole alone.

After eating, everyone remained in the big kitchen talking around the scarred mahogany table that had once been Ally's mother's pride and joy. Glad the meal was over, Ally pushed her chair from the table and stretched out her legs, slouching as a wave of weariness swept over her.

Like many of the homes in the area, the Cabrerra ranch house was built of thick limestone blocks, excavated by the earliest settlers well over a hundred years ago. A bathroom complete with claw tub had been added in the thirties; a gas stove had replaced the wood-burning one in the fifties. Since then, not much else had been done to the place. Ally had worked hard the past week, cleaning the ranch house and trying—with limited success—to brighten the old kitchen by bringing in flowers and replacing the dingy curtains with crisp white ones she'd bought with money skimmed from the grocery allowance. Nothing, however, could hide the chips in the yellow tile counters, or the battered condition of the cupboard doors.

When she caught Emma Mae looking critically at the cracked linoleum on the floor, Ally said a shade defensively, "We're redoing the whole kitchen, you know. Right after the next stock sale."

Cole frowned at her across the table, shaking his head, and Ally tilted her head inquiringly in return. Did he want their plans to remain a secret for some reason? If so, tough luck, because Emma declared bluntly, "I'm glad to hear it. This house can use some updating," and if Emma knew something—not to mention Sue Ellen—the whole town would soon know about it, too.

Perplexed by Cole's strange behavior, Ally remained silent as the conversation rambled from the sorry state of beef prices, to the never-ending heat, to the merits of the new computer that Cole had recently purchased to replace their old model. Only half listening, Ally was jerked from her thoughts when Emma announced she'd set up a Web site for the town.

"A Web site?" Ally repeated. She glanced at the older woman in surprise. "I didn't know you were hooked into the Internet."

"I'm not. My computer is too old. I set the Web site up on the one the O'Malleys donated to the town library. Janie helped me," Emma said, nodding at the younger woman—an action that caused Janie's cheeks to turn bright pink as everyone looked her way. Ignoring Janie's embarrassment, Emma added, "As a librarian, she knows plenty about computers. We posted all the information from the school as well as the latest issue of the *Tangleweed Times*."

Ally was impressed with the women's initiative; much less so with the O'Malleys' generosity. Unlike Sue Ellen, who chirped repeatedly, "How kind of the O'Malleys to do something so generous, so good for the town!" she didn't think a couple of thousand was that big a deal to a family worth millions. But, oh, what a difference a few thousand could make in her own life!

Possibly the Reverend had the same thought in regards to the new roof the church needed, or maybe—like Ally—he noticed the way the Cabrerra males all fell silent at the name O'Malley. In either case, he announced he and Janie needed to get home, and the small party quickly dispersed.

Guests gone, the Cabrerra brothers disappeared, too. Lincoln and Luke went to the barn to tinker with a broken ATV water pump, while Kyle rode out to check on the stock in the south pasture. Cole, as he did every evening, retreated to the study.

Ally was left with the cleaning up. She glanced around the kitchen, shaking her head, her mouth tightening. When needed, she helped brand, sort, feed and work cattle. She knew how to shoe the horses and mend a fence. But while it would never occur to any of her brothers to stand idly by while she worked outside on the ranch, it also never occurred to any of them to volunteer to pitch in with the often less physical but more tedious chores in the house. And lately when she asked for help, their attitude was so much of someone doing her a favor, that she preferred to just do it all herself.

So she set to work putting away the leftover food, wiping the chipped tile countertops and table and doing the dishes. Once finished, she hesitated, absently straightening the damp towel hanging beneath the farmhouse sink as she glanced out the window. The searing sun was setting, easing the harsh daytime heat. She longed to saddle up old Boomer and go for an evening ride, explore the dry riverbed or maybe catch up with Kyle to check the progress the boys had made mending the fence in the southwest pasture. Instead, she put a slice of cobbler on a plate and resolutely headed in search of Cole.

When she reached the study, she paused, leaning her shoulder against the doorjamb. Seated behind their father's big carved desk, her oldest brother was staring unseeingly out the window at the same view she'd admired a few minutes earlier. Although evening had edged in, the light filtering through the wavy glass was still bright enough to highlight the faint lines etched beside his eyes, the creases in his lean, tanned cheeks and the stern set of his mouth.

He wasn't smiling; he rarely smiled anymore, Ally realized. He'd always been rather serious, but at least he used to be more approachable. It had been big brother Cole whom Ally had run to after their mother had suddenly died in a horseback riding accident when Ally was only four. And twenty-year-old Cole who'd comforted her when their father, after a long heartrending battle, finally succumbed to lung cancer when she was fourteen.

Remembering those dark times, Ally sighed, and Cole glanced at her. His blue eyes softened as he saw the plate in her hands.

"Come to fatten me up, Al?" he asked as she walked toward him.

"I noticed you didn't have dessert earlier." She set the plate on a pile of papers littering the big desk. "And you might as well enjoy some while you can, because when we start the kitchen remodeling—"

"Actually," Cole interrupted her, "I wanted to talk to you about that. We're going to have to wait with the kitchen."

Ally sank in the chair in front of the desk to stare at him in dismay. "Why?"

"Because we just don't have the money right now to start a

major project on the house." Reading the disappointment in her expression, he added apologetically, "I was going to discuss it with you, but I just couldn't seem to find the right time."

Her lips tightened. "You mean you couldn't find the right way to tell me that the new kitchen that was so all-fired important when you were planning on bringing a wife home became considerably less so when it came to your sister."

"That's not the way it was at all," he said, deep voice sharpening defensively. "I knew we had to have a new computer—" he nodded at the machine that sat center stage, glowing softly on the broad oak desk "—but I didn't expect to have to replace the engine on the pickup this year as well as get another baler. You know we can't do without either of those, and the new computer will make charting the breeding records, as well as doing the books, a hundred times faster and easier."

"And buying a new stove and dishwasher would make my work a hundred times faster and easier, too." Ally shook her head in frustration. "For goodness' sake, Cole, the oven door falls off every time I open it too far. Do you know how hard it is to pull out a pan of hot biscuits with one hand, while trying to keep the oven door on with the other?"

"Okay, I'm sorry." He sighed, running a hand through his thick dark hair. "I'll get Luke or Linc to weld a new hinge on it. And as soon as we can afford it, I'll buy you a new stove. I promise."

Ally wasn't impressed with his assurance. "If you let Vorquez go, we could afford the stove right now."

Ally knew that George Vorquez, the land claims man Cole had hired to prospect for oil, was one of the most respected geologists in the county. But if their father, who had the Circle C tested years ago, hadn't met with success, she doubted they'd have any now.

But Cole's jaw tightened. He picked up his fork and moodily stabbed at the crust of the cobbler. "Oil's there, Al. I know it is.

It just takes time and a bit of money to find it. And then we'll be richer than we ever dreamed of being."

"So instead of putting in a new kitchen, you're taking a gamble that we'll find oil."

"It isn't a gamble, Ally," Cole said firmly. "It's an investment."

"Fine. Whatever." Ally refused to argue with him on a subject she knew he wouldn't budge on. "The point is, Cole, you're not being fair to me."

"I said we'll fix the stove—"

"Yeah, when someone gets around to it." Her lips compressed. "Besides, it's not just that. It's other things, too."

"Like what?"

"Like…" She tried to think of a recent example. "Like when you got the cell phones. You gave one to Kyle, one to each of the twins and kept the other one for yourself. Without discussing it with me at all."

"I wasn't trying to slight you, Al. The plan just came with four, so I handed them out to the boys, and figured you could share with me."

"I don't want to share with you. I want my own."

"But why? Who are you planning on calling?"

"No one," she admitted, giving up on the battle. "And there's no one planning to call me."

His face softened. "Sure there is. Tell you what—you can have the cell. I'll share with Kyle."

She looked at him helplessly. He just didn't get it. The problem was, she didn't want to always feel like Cole—or the others—were doing her a favor. She wanted them to recognize that she worked just as hard as they did. That she'd earned her share.

"It's not the phone, Cole. It's that you don't treat me like an equal. You don't discuss anything with me. Not anything concerning the ranch or the house. Not even Bride's Price."

Cole's frowning eyes lifted to meet hers. "What about it?"

"Don't you think you should have consulted me before refusing Troy's offer?"

Cole shifted his gaze back to the cobbler. He gave it another poke. "No."

"That's my land, Cole."

Setting his fork aside, he lifted his dark eyebrows as he met her eyes once again. "No one says it isn't. But I'm the one Eileen put in charge to look out for your best interests."

Ally folded her arms across her chest. "And that's what you were doing today? Protecting my interests?"

"Of course. What else would I be doing? We need that grass for the herd."

"Don't give me that. We have more than enough range for the herd we're running now. You know and I know that if anyone else had wanted to lease that land, you would have agreed in a red-hot minute. The only reason you refused is because it was Troy O'Malley."

Cole's stern mouth curled in a grim smile. "Seems like a good enough reason to me."

"Well, not to me."

His smile faded and his blue gaze narrowed on her face. "Since when have you become so concerned about Troy O'Malley?"

She gave a short laugh, waving a dismissing hand at the thought of mocking green eyes. "I'm not concerned with him at all. What I want—what I need—is that money he offered. To put my own plans into action."

"What plans?"

"To move into Eileen's house."

Cole snorted. "You're kidding me. Why would you want to move out there?"

"To be able to do what I want."

Genuinely perplexed, Cole frowned at her. "That's ridiculous. What can you do at Eileen's house that you can't do here?"

I could paint the place pink, hang lace curtains at all the windows if I decide to, without anyone groaning about it. I wouldn't have to clean up constantly after four messy men. I could put on lipstick and eye shadow—experiment with makeup—without being teased that I look like a rodeo clown. I could take hour-long baths without an irritable male pounding on the door asking "Have you died in there?" And I could go out on dates, stay out all night if I choose to, without one or all of my four brothers intimidating the hell out of the poor guy I'd gone out with.

She was fed up with being the fifth, inferior Cabrerra brother, Ally realized tiredly. She just wanted to be by herself—run her own life, make her own decisions—without any bossy men telling her what she should and shouldn't do.

But Cole wouldn't understand any of that; he'd simply dismiss it as female nonsense. So Ally gave him a reason he could understand. "I want to start my own business. Breeding and training horses."

Cole's expression tightened. "That's a dream, Ally. There's no money in that." Impatiently, he shook his head. "Cattle is our concern."

"Our major concern. I want to start a side business, breeding and training Peruvian Pasos for working herds and pleasure riding."

"Peruvian Pasos," he repeated flatly. "What's wrong with good old American quarter horses?"

She shrugged. "Nothing. But I want to develop Peruvians."

He took a deep breath, clearly summoning patience. "Fine. But we can't afford to support two households right now, or invest in more horses. Maybe in a few years—"

"I don't want to wait a few years, any more than you want to wait years to find out if there's oil on our land. Not if I don't have to. And leasing to Troy means that I don't have to."

"I'm not leasing Bride's Price to Troy O'Malley."

Ally's spine stiffened, and her gaze narrowed on her brother's stubborn face. "No?" she asked softly. "Is that because he's an O'Malley? Or because he stole Misty from you?"

She shouldn't have said it; Ally regretted the comment as soon as it left her lips. Cole jerked as if she'd slapped him and his expression turned to stone.

When he finally replied, he didn't answer her questions but stated in a flat, hard voice he'd never used to her before, "O'Malley is not getting that lease. And there's nothing you can do about it."

Not waiting for her reply, he stood and strode from the room, slamming the door behind him.

Ally sat for a moment, frozen in place by the force of his anger, hurt constricting her throat and causing a prickly burning behind her eyes.

Then an answering anger rose up inside her. Blinking the pain away, she glared at the closed door.

"Oh, yes, there is something I can do, brother dear," she said softly. "I can get married."

Chapter Two

"During the breeding season, it is wise to observe the cattle from a distance, using field glasses if necessary, to remain unseen and thus avoid influencing their natural behavior.

"Don't hesitate to enlist the aid of other experts in this endeavor. They may have knowledge that you lack…."
— *Successful Breeding: A Guide for the Cattleman*

Resolving to marry was one thing; finding a husband quite another. Especially if all the single men in town were intimidated by your four older brothers.

Well, she simply had to overcome that obstacle, Ally decided, lying in bed that night, pondering the problem. What she needed to do was get close enough to her prospect—once she had a prospect—to explain her proposition of a temporary marriage before her brothers could chase him off. Getting dressed up would help her get close. Every woman over the age of five knew that men—like bulls—were easily distracted and attracted by clothing. Flutter a red cape—or a sexy red dress—in front of them, and they almost couldn't help chasing it.

The trouble was, she didn't have a red dress—or any sexy clothes—nor the money to buy some. The only decent dress she owned was her bridesmaid dress from Cole's canceled wedding…a dress she'd never worn.

Yes, that was the answer, she decided, settling down to get some sleep. She'd return the dress and get something new.

Her brothers headed out at dawn the next morning. After they left, Ally hurried to clean up the breakfast dishes, feed the chickens and start a load of laundry—sparing a few extra moments to flush the cigarettes she found in Kyle's pocket. Bad enough that he risked his life riding bulls; he didn't need to risk cancer, too.

Anxious to reach Tangleweed when the stores opened, she was on the road at nine. By ten, she was arguing with Tammy Pitts, owner of Tamara's Treasures.

"I'm sorry, I can't refund your money," Tammy said.

"But I've never worn it," Ally told her. "It's like new."

"Doesn't matter," Tammy insisted. "Not only has it been six months since you purchased the garment, it was altered. It can't be returned." She pushed the dress across the store counter, adding with patently false regret, "Store policy, you know. One my *regular* customers completely understand."

The condescending glance she swept over Ally's worn jeans and John Deere T-shirt—clean and green and bought on sale at the feed store—made Ally lift her chin. Ally had known Tammy Pitts (née Peale) all her life. After trapping William Pitts, a man twice her age, into marriage, Tammy had convinced her henpecked husband to let her open a boutique which—since most of the town refused to pay the prices Tammy charged—primarily served as a front for Tammy's shopping addiction.

But when planning her wedding to Cole, Misty'd been determined to give her hometown as much business as possible. So she'd herded her bridesmaids to Tamara's Treasures. Although the others had been dismayed by Tammy's "hick-town slim pickin's," as one anorexic redhead had put it, Ally's only dismay had been the cost of the final selection. Emptying her small savings account for a dress she'd probably wear once had scandalized her thrifty soul. But she'd bitten back her protests, not wanting to embarrass either herself or Cole in front of the other women, for whom price was obviously not a consideration at all.

Serves me right for not speaking up then, Ally thought bitterly. *Because sure as stink on a cross-eyed skunk I'm going to be embarrassed, anyway, once Tammy tells everyone in town that I tried to return the dress.*

Before she could grab the dress and escape, the bell above the door to the shop chimed.

Tammy directed a broad smile at the person entering. "Hello, Misty," Tammy said, then glanced at Ally with speculative interest.

Ally turned to see Misty Sanderson hovering in the doorway, looking as startled to see Ally, as Ally was to see her. Although they were the same age, Ally had never known the petite blonde very well, since rather than the public school in Tangleweed Ally had attended, Raymond Sanderson had sent his only daughter to a private boarding school in the east.

During Misty's engagement to Cole, the two women had become friends but Ally loved her brother—warts and all—and she couldn't forgive the blonde for the pain she'd caused him. So neither woman had seen the other since the breakup.

For a fleeting second, Ally thought Misty would ignore her

now. But after the barest hesitation, Misty smiled briefly at Ally, then returned Tammy's greeting with a casual hello.

"I've come to pick up that jacket I ordered. Has it come in yet?" Misty asked Tammy as she walked toward the counter.

"Oh, yes. It's in the rear." Tammy's inquisitive gaze flicked from Misty's face to Ally's, before she added with obvious reluctance, "I'll go get it."

As soon as the sharp tippety-tip-tap of Tammy's high heels faded in the back room, Misty turned to Ally, asking politely, "How are you, Ally?"

"I'm fine," Ally responded in the same tone. "And you?"

"Doing great," Misty said emphatically, widening her lips in a smile that didn't quite reach her dark brown eyes. "I've been busy, what with—" Her smile faltered as she recognized the dress on the counter. "Oh! It's your bridesmaid dress." She looked at Ally, tilting her head questioningly. "Why did you bring it here?"

"I'm returning it," Ally said bluntly, as she started to bundle the blue froth of material into her arms. Not bothering to soften her tone she added, "I don't need it, after all, since there's never going to be a wedding. Not between you and Cole, anyway."

Misty stared at her while the tippety-tip-tap signaling Tammy's return grew louder. Then suddenly her face crumpled. She whirled toward the door.

Shaken by the raw anguish in Misty's eyes, Ally dropped her dress to chase after her. Misty sped outside and Ally reached the door just as Tammy called out, "Wait! Where y'all going?"

"To get coffee."

She caught up with Misty in front of Virgil's Hardware two stores away, and grasped the other girl's arm to stop her, aghast at the sight of the tears on Misty's cheeks. Misty had always appeared so sophisticated and in control to Ally. And smiling—

Ally couldn't remember a time when perky Misty had been sad or upset. But Misty was definitely upset now. Sobs shook her slender shoulders as she leaned against the hardware's brick siding, tears seeping from beneath the trembling hand she'd lifted to cover her eyes.

Ally felt terrible. "I'm sorry, Misty," she said softly. Not knowing what else to do and afraid Tammy would appear at any moment, she added, "Look, can we go someplace and talk? Have coffee?"

Misty hesitated, then nodded.

Breathing a sigh of relief, Ally steered the smaller girl toward the truck she'd parked a few yards away. Ally unlocked the passenger door for Misty to climb in, then went around to the driver's side. Once inside, Ally rolled down her window to relieve some of the relentless heat, and Misty listlessly followed suit as Ally started the motor and put the truck in gear. They traveled the four blocks up Main Street to Daisy's Diner, passing the Deer Processing Plant and the bank without exchanging a word.

When they reached the diner, Ally parked beneath a withered pecan growing by the curb. The shade of the tree was welcome, easing the heat, and for a minute or two after Ally cut the motor, the two sat while a hot breeze drifted through the cab, Misty cried, and Ally tried to decide what to do.

She glanced over as Misty sat up a little straighter to open the handbag in her lap. The blonde fumbled around inside, then pulled out a tissue to stem the tears still trickling from her eyes. It didn't help; the tears kept coming, and the sight of her obvious distress finally shattered the reserve Ally'd been determined to maintain.

"If you still care so much, Misty," she blurted out, "then why did you break up with him?"

"Is that what he said?" Misty whipped around to face her so fiercely that Ally shrank involuntarily against the door. "That I broke up with *him?* Because if he did, your brother is nothing but a *liar!*"

The door handle was gouging Ally's back but she stayed put, alarmed by the hot flare of anger in Misty's eyes. "Yes—well, no. Cole never talked about it. I just assumed—"

"You just assumed I was the kind of woman who would dump a man on a whim weeks before the wedding." Misty's lips quivered and she pressed them firmly together. "Well, I didn't. I love—loved Cole with all my heart. There was nothing I wanted in this world more than to be his wife."

The sorrow in Misty's voice, the hopeless yearning in her face, was unmistakable.

Ally said helplessly, "But I know Cole loves you...."

"Apparently not." Bitterness tainted Misty's sweet Texas twang as she added, "Or at least, not enough to marry me."

"But he does, I know he does," Ally insisted. "I just don't understand why he broke up with you."

"Oh, don't you? Well, his excuse was Troy O'Malley." Misty blew her little nose defiantly. "He refused to believe me when I assured him there's nothing at all romantic between Troy and me."

She must have seen the doubt on Ally's face because she added impatiently, "Yes, there's a bond between us. After all, Troy's father was killed in the same car accident as my mother, and that's always been a tragedy we shared. And he had to go away to boarding school, too. In some respects Troy's been—been like a brother to me. But there is nothing, never has been and never will be, *anything* romantic between us," she said fiercely, meeting Ally's glance with a burning brown gaze that refused to waver. "Believe me, because I've never meant anything more."

"I believe you." Ally did—concerning Misty's feelings, any-way. But as to how Troy might feel about Misty...

"Thank you, Ally." Misty smiled at her and, reaching over, gave Ally's hand an impulsive squeeze. "I just wish that stubborn brother of yours had believed in me, too."

"Maybe if you try again—"

"I refuse to take the blame for something I didn't do. He refused to even listen to me. He'd made up his mind and that was that." Determined pride lifted Misty's chin, but hurt was clear in her eyes as she added, "Besides, like I said, Troy was just an excuse. What Cole really can't tolerate is the fact that my daddy is rich."

Ally drew a troubled breath, unable to deny that Misty was probably right. "Cole can be stubborn," she admitted.

"No kidding." Misty gave an unamused laugh and swiped rather savagely at the dampness lingering on her cheeks. "I don't know why I'm even crying over the mule-headed male. What's past is past, and heaven knows, I have more important things to worry about like—" Impulsively she turned to face Ally, her eyes glimmering with tears once more. "Oh, Ally, my daddy is sick. Really sick."

Ally's throat tightened in sympathy. "Is it his heart again?"

Misty nodded. "The doctors aren't saying much, but—" She choked back a sob and gave Ally an apologetic look. "I didn't mean to blurt all this out. No one knows. It would hurt his business badly—our stock would plummet even more than it has. You know how it is…"

Ally nodded. She did know. Raymond Sanderson *was* his company. Without him, Sanderson Technology would most likely cease to exist. "I'm sorry."

Misty forced a smile. "No, I'm sorry—about crying and all. It's just, since I can't talk to anyone about it, I guess I get scared sometimes and feel kind of alone—but Daddy will be *fine*," she said stoutly. "I know he will."

"I'm sure he will, too," Ally agreed, with more certainty than she felt. "And you can talk to me anytime. Really. I promise I won't say a word, not to anyone. But, Misty, if Cole knew you're having trouble—"

"No!" Misty turned fierce again, her petite figure immediately stiffening. "If he didn't want me before, I certainly don't want his pity now."

Ally understood how Misty felt. If Cole loved Misty—and Ally was sure he did—then it was up to him to reach out to her.

But she felt sorry for Misty. Losing a parent was hard at any time, but Misty was all alone. At least Ally had had her brothers. Especially Cole.

"I just don't know what's gotten into Cole lately," she said, worrying aloud.

"What do you mean?" Misty asked, her dark eyes still bright from her tears.

Ally hadn't intended to tell anyone about her plans to gain control of Bride's Price. But her remorse at hurting Misty, her sympathy about Misty's father and the knowledge that the other woman cared about Cole and had confided in her, had Ally explaining her own dilemma in return.

By the time she finished, Misty was wide-eyed with amazement. "You really intend to do it? Ask some guy to marry you?"

"What other choice do I have?"

"None, if Cole won't budge—and I doubt that he will. But still…how long do you need to stay married?"

"I'm not sure," Ally admitted. "Not long at all if Cole gives in, I suppose. If he doesn't, then at least long enough for him to legally be removed as trustee for Bride's Price. Whether that happens immediately upon the marriage, I don't know. Do you?"

"Haven't a clue," Misty admitted.

Ally sighed. "I guess I'll have to find out from a lawyer.

Before I do that, I want to line up some guy to help me out. Maybe, if he sees I'm serious, Cole will back down and I can save the lawyer's fee."

"Or Cole'll convince the guy to back down," Misty prophesied dryly. "Or one of your other brothers will. You have to admit, they can be formidable."

"Yeah, but I'm hoping money might make the difference. I thought I'd offer some of the lease money Troy's willing to pay as incentive to my prospective groom."

Misty looked impressed. "That's a good idea. Who are you thinking of asking?"

"I'm not sure yet. Maybe Dave Sarten."

Misty shook her head. "He just got engaged to Pam Watkins. What about Jack Ryder?"

"He got a job managing a ranch up in South Dakota. Left last week. I was thinking maybe Travis Wesley…"

"Nope. He's got a steady girlfriend in Abilene. Buck Boulter might do it, except—"

"He's good friends with Cole," Ally finished for her.

They lapsed into gloomy silence, staring out the bug-splattered windshield. The cab was hot and smelled like cigarettes, gasoline and rotting vegetables—not too overwhelming when driving, but not especially pleasant when sitting in the blazing sun.

Misty picked up a crumpled fast-food bag by her feet. She looked inside, and wrinkled her nose. "So that's what stinks. These fries are just about petrified. Ally, your brothers—"

"I know," Ally said glumly, batting at a fat fly that wandered in. "They're all slobs."

Misty tossed the bag over the seat. "You let them get away with too much. You need to—" She tensed, her eyes widening as she stared past Ally's shoulder at someone across the street. "Hey, Ally! What about him?"

Ally turned and lifted her hand, shading her eyes against the sun as she studied the figure walking away. "Dwayne Cronk?" she asked doubtfully. "I guess, since he just bags groceries at the Piggly Wiggly he could probably use the money, but he always smells like cooked cabbage—"

"Not him—*him!* The guy who bought the Laundromat and turned it into that antique store! What's his name? Tim? Tom?"

"Theodore—Theodore Bayor," Ally told her, a vague memory surfacing. She squinted to read the fancy gold-and-black script scrawled on the store window across the street. "Of Bayor's Antiques and Collectibles. What about him?"

Misty's face shone with enthusiasm. "He'd be perfect! After all, he's new in town, and Tammy told me that though the store's been open two months now it isn't making much—so he probably needs the money."

Ally studied the man arranging a pair of silver candlesticks in the store's front window. His face was hidden by a dark brown mustache and full beard, but judging by the thick, curly brown hair on his head and his athletic build—wide shoulders, lean hips—he appeared to be in his late twenties or early thirties. "Are you sure he isn't married?"

"Tammy says he bought the store with an elderly woman named Mrs. Bayor—that must be his mother, over there." Misty pointed out a plump, gray-haired woman about seventy or so in a dark dress, standing behind a counter. "Tammy told me they're both from California. It's just the two of them, so he's obviously used to working with a woman and— Oh, hide! Quick! He's looking this way!"

The girls ducked. Misty made the move with smooth grace, but Ally's longer legs got in the way and she whacked her knee on the dashboard. "Ouch!"

"Shush!" Misty commanded.

They stayed slouched a few seconds in frozen silence. Then Ally said dryly, "Did we really need to hide?"

Misty gave a small chuckle. "I panicked," she admitted. "But we don't want him to see us sit back up—that might look suspicious."

She glanced at Ally. "Anyway, like I was saying, if he's used to working with his mother, he shouldn't have any problem working with you. Here—" She groped around the floor and came up with the binoculars the boys kept in the truck. "Uck! They're sticky," she complained. She wiped the lenses gingerly with her crumpled tissue, then held them up to her eyes to take another look. "He's not bad-looking. At least he doesn't resemble his mother. Why, the poor woman's three plucked hairs short of a unibrow. Take a look."

She passed the glasses over, and Ally peered at Theodore's mother. Misty was right; the woman's thick, dark brows almost met over the bridge of her long nose.

"And," Misty added, as Ally slunk back beneath the window's edge, "he can't be intimidated by your brothers, 'cause he doesn't know them."

"He's met Linc and Luke," Ally pointed out. "Luke's the one who mentioned him awhile back. He said the new guy is pretty good at pool, so I guess he plays Friday nights at Big Bob's. They've never mentioned getting in a fight with him, though."

"There you go!" Misty exclaimed, as if that clinched the matter. "What else do you need?"

Lifting the glasses, Ally chanced another peek. He was looking the other way, so she studied his face. He had thick dark hair and nice-enough eyes, she decided. Like Misty said, not bad looking at all, unlike his mother. Ally pointed the glasses Mrs. Bayor's way—and found her glaring back.

"Damn!" Ally quickly ducked, guiltily dropping the binoculars. "I think his mother saw me."

Misty checked. "No. She's still cleaning." She glanced at
Ally. "So? What do you think?"

"He's okay," Ally admitted. "And, anyway, beggars can't be
choosers. Do you think I should just go in there and ask him now?
Forget about getting dressed up?"

"No," Misty said decisively. "Dressing up is always good.
Besides, you don't want to corner him, especially on his own ter-
ritory—and with his mother watching, too. Better to approach
him on neutral ground—like Big Bob's bar on Friday!" she
declared, beaming with sudden inspiration. Then she frowned.
"No, wait, you said the twins hang out there."

"They used to. They're banned for fighting."

"What about Kyle? Or…Cole?"

Hearing the diffident note in Misty's tone, Ally assured her,
"Cole never goes out." Happy to see Misty's tense expression
ease, Ally added, "And Kyle's been going to Abilene every
weekend. He must be seeing someone there."

Misty smiled, saying again, "There you go, then. We'll get
you dressed up in something so sexy, you won't have to approach
Theodore, he'll come to you. And even if he doesn't, we'll shake
someone out of the woodwork," she added on a practical note.

Ally smiled wryly. That might be true for Misty, who even
with mascara smudged beneath her eyes, tearstains smeared on
her cheeks, and her designer blouse wrinkled, still looked
feminine and sweet. Unlike Ally, who felt sweaty and worn-out
from her sleepless night. And all her T-shirt was likely to attract
was a tractor fanatic. "I don't have anything sexy. And since
Tammy won't take the dress back—"

"Oh, pooh on Tammy" Misty said darkly. "She's never getting

my business again." Apparently forgetting they were hiding, she straightened indignantly in her seat.

Ally slowly sat up, too. She glanced toward the antique store. Mrs. Bayor was staring directly at them. Misty saw her and waggled her fingers cheerfully. Ally waved tentatively, too. Mrs. Bayor scowled harder.

Ally hastily turned toward Misty, who'd opened her door to jump out of the truck. "Let's get some coffee, collect your dress from Tammy, and then you can follow me to my house," Misty suggested. "I'll lend you an outfit that'll be so smokin', the men at Big Bob's will gather round you like Scouts at a campfire, eager for a weenie roast."

Ally tried to protest. "Honestly, Misty, men never think I'm hot."

"They will when I get through with you," Misty promised. She wrinkled her nose ruefully, adding, "You're taller than me, but we're about the same size other than that, I think. I have a cute skirt you can borrow, and a darling blouse. And I have a wig you can borrow, too."

"A wig?" Ally repeated doubtfully. "Won't that make me look like I'm in a costume?"

"Not this wig," Misty said confidently. "It cost almost as much as a small car. I wear it all the time when my hair won't behave and no one knows it's a wig at all."

"Yeah, but you're a blonde," Ally said, feeling compelled to point out the obvious. "I'm a brunette."

Misty airily waved that aside. "So you'll be blonde for a night. Believe me, nothing alters a woman's appearance more dramatically—or gathers more male attention—than changing your hair color." She pondered for a moment, then amended, "Except, maybe, showing off your cleavage. Or your legs. Or your bottom in a tight skirt." She nodded decisively. "And we'll do all that, too. Or at least—" her engaging grin dawned "—*you* will."

Panic fluttered in Ally's stomach. "Wait a minute. I'm not sure—"

"Don't worry," Misty said. "When it comes to getting fixed up, I *am* sure. So be prepared to sizzle."

Chapter Three

"When evaluating a bull for stud, after testicle size, the next item to consider is the behavioral health of the animal. Is he unwontedly distracted by males in the vicinity?

"A bull whose territorial instincts are overly developed will need to be kept separate from other males. Otherwise, his energy will be expended in fighting, rather than in mating…."
—*Successful Breeding: A Guide for the Cattleman*

Troy Michael O'Malley had a definite fondness for Big Bob's Bar and Grill.

Not because the place was at all attractive. Like its owner Big Bob Gallarza—who couldn't beat a bull dog in a beauty contest—the outside of the barnlike building was worn and weathered. Inside, a scarred mesquite bar dominated one end of the long, smoky room, while three billiard tables on which "Do or Die" tournaments were featured every Friday night jammed up the middle. To hide his lack of cleaning skills, Big Bob scattered straw over the peanut shells on the wooden plank floor, and diners—if eating at Big Bob's could be termed dining—were squeezed in at small tables at the back, disconcertingly close to the doors marked "Gents" and "Gals" in chipped gilt lettering.

Yet, despite its lack of ambience, Big Bob's Bar and Grill did plenty of business, simply by featuring the four essential "b's" of the typical Texas male: booze, beef, babes and barbecue sauce. The booze Big Bob plunked down on his scarred mesquite bar came at reasonable prices, and the steaks were thick and reasonable, too. The majority of the rodeo bunnies perched on the bar stools were also reasonable; just out for a good time with a big-buckled cowboy.

But far and away what made Big Bob's place *really* special— at least in Troy's opinion—was the barbecue sauce. After all, booze, babes and a decent steak could be found anywhere in Texas—anywhere in the world, for that matter, from run-down cantinas in Tijuana, to exclusive resorts in the Swiss Alps. But nowhere else could a man find sauces like Hot Pecos, Lil Red's, Risky Rita's, Babalou and dozens more, all crowded—neck to shiny bottleneck—on Big Bob's pint-size tables.

Seated in a shadowy corner, Troy studied the impressive array of colorful bottles before him. He pushed aside a yellow No Butts, and a blue Eagle Eye, searching for—ah, there it was!— Smokin' Jo's, his longtime favorite.

Picking up the tall brown bottle, Troy hefted it in his hand, gazing fondly at the smoking six-gun pictured on the yellow label. This was the sauce he'd tipped back his chair to recommend to a redhead and her two friends at a nearby table a couple of Friday nights ago. He'd been bored, and the flirty, knowing expression on the redhead's face as she considered his sauce boded well as a distraction for the evening.

Until Luke Cabrerra horned in with a recommendation of his own.

"Smokin' Jo's?" Luke had declared with an exaggerated, good ole boy drawl and an equally exaggerated lift of his eyebrows. Turning from the pool table where he'd been shooting against his twin, Luke rested his stick on the floor while he'd eyed the bottle in the redhead's hand. With a reproving shake of his dark head, he'd said to her, "I don't think so. Not for a sweet little thing like you. Quick Draw is more your style," he added, reaching over her shoulder to pick up a slim green bottle. Looking at the label, Luke read as if quoting Scripture, "'Best barbecue sauce west of the Atlantic and east of the Pacific.' Now this is a sauce with *kick*."

"Kick?" Hell, if Luke Cabrerra wanted kick, Troy would be glad to oblige—by kicking the other man's ass. Relishing the task, Troy rose to step closer to the woman, also. And when Cabrerra bent over the table to offer his selection to her, Troy leaned over the table, too, and gently but firmly pushed the green bottle aside.

"C'mon, Cabrerra," he said. "Don't insult the lady. She's looking for something that'll make her toes curl. Something hot, yet smooth and satisfying. Something that will leave her with a warm glow inside. Like Smokin' Jo's."

Troy earned a flutter of the redhead's false eyelashes and giggles from her friends in reward, but before he could press his advantage, there went Cabrerra, butting in again.

"Smooth and satisfying?" Luke snorted, leaning in closer. "Everyone knows Smokin' Jo's is all bitch and no bite. Why, that sauce is so thick it takes forever to get out of the bottle."

Troy leaned in closer, too. "So?" he said softly. "Who wants a sauce that's so weak, it pours out after one small shake?" He added deliberately, "Like yours does."

Luke stiffened. Flinging down his pool cue, he clenched his fists, demanding through gritted teeth, "Are you saying my sauce has no staying power?"

"Ya got it."

Cabrerra had lunged then—or maybe Troy had. He wasn't really sure. All he knew was that by the time the sheriff arrived, beer, blood and barbecue sauce were scattered everywhere.

The redhead and her friends had scattered, too. Troy hadn't seen her since and he had a sneaky suspicion she wouldn't be back. It didn't really matter. What mattered was that although Luke was a bit younger and a bit taller than Troy—and neither had ever quit swinging—Troy figured he'd won the fight. After all, as he'd pointed out to Luke as they were led away by the sheriff, *Troy's* barbecue bottle had made it through the melee unbroken, while Luke's—weak as it was—had been reduced to a thin, red puddle on the floor.

Shaking his head in remembered pity for the other man's humiliation, Troy upended Smokin' Jo's over his steak and gave the bottle a couple of firm taps. Half a minute later, he administered a couple more. Okay, so maybe the sauce *was* thick. That wasn't necessarily a bad thing—not for a man with patience. And Troy had plenty of patience. All the O'Malleys had when it came to getting something they wanted.

He hit the bottle again. Take his grandfather, for example. For more than sixty years Old Mick had waited to get back Bride's Price from the Cabrerras. Troy was determined the old man wouldn't wait one more year—one more month, if possible—for his lifelong goal to come true. Not only for Mick's sake, but for Troy's, as well.

Because ranching, like bull riding, was in Troy's blood— what he'd been born to do. And Mick had finally—*finally*— agreed to honor the promise he'd made when Troy was a kid, to turn the management of the huge family spread over to Troy.

Just as soon as Troy handed over the deed to Bride's Price.

Yep, Mick was holding up his side of the bargain. "I've put my lawyer on to it," he'd told Troy just a week ago. "You'll have controlling interest in the Running M in a couple of weeks, and as soon as you close the deal on that other damn property, I'll tell that new foreman I hired he'll have to move on."

Troy slapped his bottle. Mick should have had Bride's Price back already—*would* have had it if Eileen Hennessey hadn't died before Troy had gotten her agreement to sell in black and white. Although he hadn't expected to, the better he'd gotten to know the old gal, the more he'd liked her. They'd become friends. She'd wanted to sell to him. Trust the Cabrerra siblings, stubborn idiots that they were, to refuse to believe it.

Troy slapped the bottle harder. Smokin' Jo's grudgingly oozed a millimeter farther down the neck, so Troy added shaking to his tapping, keeping time to the Willie Nelson song bawling over the speakers. The bar was packed with cowboys in town for the next day's rodeo, with even more streaming in. Still tapping, Troy glanced idly toward the entrance—just as Misty Sanderson sashayed through Big Bob's prized swinging doors.

Troy paused in his sauce decanting, sure for a moment he must be mistaken. That it had to be some other woman with similar shoulder-length, kinda tousled-looking blond hair. He'd *never* seen Misty in here on a Friday night after ten before—or any other night of the week, for that matter. Misty Sanderson was downtown Dallas, not down-home Big Bob's Bar and Grill. But the woman was dressed Misty-style in a yellow silk blouse that managed to look sexy and elegant at the same time, butt-hugging blue jeans and—to clinch the matter—cowboy boots. Misty's all-time weakness was designer cowboy boots, the gawd-awful gaudier the better, and this little pair was made of bright blue leather, splattered with gold Texas stars. As the blonde pranced toward the bar in them, a dim overhead light slid across smooth high cheekbones, big brown eyes and an unmistakable sweet smile. Yeah, it was Misty, all right.

Unthinkingly, Troy set down Smokin' Jo's—thus losing the little bit of momentum the sauce had started to attain—to watch as she gestured to a woman trailing a few steps behind. Another blonde. Half a head taller than Misty but just as slim, this one's hair was shorter, curving smoothly to just below her slender jawline. Her sleeveless red blouse was modest enough, but the denim skirt she had on was pretty damn daring—short and tight enough to raise women's eyebrows and men's hopes. Misty's friend must have felt it was a little risky, too, because she tugged at the hem every few steps or so, futilely trying to pull it lower on her thighs.

Troy narrowed his eyes, studying those shapely thighs. He wasn't much good with faces, but he was great with legs. And he couldn't imagine forgetting those long, tanned, sexy limbs displayed to such advantage in that short denim skirt. Slender, firm thighs. Nice calves. Delicate ankles. Pretty feet in flat leather sandals that weren't much more than soles and a couple of straps.

Yeah, he'd definitely seen Short Skirt before.

Even the way she moved seemed familiar. While Misty strode confidently ahead with that shoulders-back, chin-held-high glide she'd learned in the East Coast boarding school she'd attended, Short Skirt moved much slower. Clutching a red purse strap against her high, shapely breasts, she took each step gracefully, yet almost warily, too, as she followed her friend. Like a deer approaching a water hole at dusk during the hunting season.

And this little darlin' had plenty of reason to tread warily. More males had noticed the women. Danny Wilson, bending to shoot at the tables, straightened and gave the newcomers a thorough once-over. Ralph Henderson, standing nearby, pulled his ball cap lower on his bald head, and hitched the waist of his Wranglers a shade higher over his paunchy beer belly. At the next table, Theodore Bayor completely missed his shot.

Misty, occupied with claiming a couple of empty bar stools next to a chubby stranger in a green plaid shirt, seemed oblivious to the rising testosterone flooding the room. But her friend remained uneasy, still looking around as she joined the smaller blonde. And when she reached her bar stool, Short Skirt hesitated a second before climbing up.

Troy grinned when she couldn't make it on the first try. That skirt was just too damn tight. His amusement deepened as she gave a more determined hop and landed on the leather seat. While she composed herself, setting her purse on the bar and wiggling her pert butt to get more comfortable on the stool, Misty started waving a slender hand in the air as if she was bidding on a vase at a Sotheby's auction, trying to get Big Bob's attention. When that didn't work, Misty stood on the rungs of her bar stool to get additional height waving even more vigorously.

His grin widening, Troy stood up to go say hi to Misty and get an introduction to her friend. But then he paused, grimaced and sat again.

His right knee hurt—had been hurting like a son of a bitch on and off for a couple of weeks. He knew he should see a doctor, but he didn't want to know if something was seriously damaged. Not until he'd placed first in the bull riding tomorrow, anyway. Until then, he'd keep managing—quite nicely, thank you—with a few shots of whiskey or beer every night, aspirin or the occasional painkiller to numb the grinding ache.

But his knee wasn't the only thing that stopped him from joining Misty; her expression kept him away, too. Because she looked so happy as she leaned over the bar. More carefree—more alive—than Troy'd seen her these past few months. And if Troy

went over there, Misty would look at him and her smile would
fade. Oh, she'd quickly replace it. But her new smile would be
strained and the dancing light in her eyes would be gone, replaced
by uncertainty and guilt.

That would make him angry and she'd know it—'cause he and
Misty were tight and they understood each other real well. His
anger would make her feel even worse, and that would make him
even angrier, and so it would go, on and on.

Reaching into his shirt pocket, Troy pulled out a small plastic
bottle and twisted off the cap. He shook the last two pain pills
into his palm, downed them, then tossed the plastic bottle aside
to reach for his whiskey. Yeah, that's exactly what would happen
if he went over to Misty; he'd bet the Running M on it. Because
that's exactly what happened every time he saw her lately.

Ever since her breakup with Cole Cabrerra.

At the thought of the oldest Cabrerra, Troy downed a shot of
whiskey, then another. Eyes watering, he glanced Misty's way.
The place was filling up fast, and since Big Bob had his hands
full handling the orders of the people crowding up to the bar,
Misty and her friend still hadn't gotten served. Nor had anyone
gotten up the nerve to approach them yet, Troy noted, although
the guy in green plaid kept shooting them sidelong glances.
Ralph looked ready to make his move, too. He hitched up his
jeans, hitched them again and took a step in Misty's direction—
then froze with his gaze fixed beyond her at the entrance and immediately returned to the pool game.

Short Skirt chose that moment to glance at the entrance, too. And,
to Troy's mild surprise, she froze just like Ralph, then hopped off
her stool. Grabbing her purse, she hurried toward the restrooms.

Troy watched her come closer, enjoying her leggy stride.
Teased again by that sense of familiarity, he waited for her to
glance his way. *Had* he seen her before? She drew nearer—he

craned his neck to see her better through the smoky gloom—but with a fleeting glance toward his shadowy corner, she turned her face away and headed straight for the "Gals" room. Shoving the door open, she disappeared inside.

Disappointed, Troy glanced toward the entrance, curious to see what had spooked everyone. For a second, flannel shirts and blue denim rears blocked his view, but then the way cleared and—speak of the devil—damned if it wasn't Cole Cabrerra standing there.

Like a heat-seeking laser, Cabrerra's gaze locked on Misty's slender figure and he started toward her. No one got in his way. One quick glance at his angry scowl had even Big Bob, who was built like a Brahman bull, moving quietly to the other end of the counter.

Cole reached Misty in less than five seconds flat. He tapped her shoulder, she turned—and for an unguarded second her face lit up. Troy's chest tightened. Then Cole said something, and her expression changed. She looked—well, *desolate* was the word that came closest in Troy's mind. Once again he started to rise, to go over to her. But before he could push his chair back, Misty's expression altered again and she straightened abruptly. Indignation radiated from her small figure. Since she was still standing on the rungs of the bar stool she just about met Cabrerra eye to eye. Her slim brows lowered, her hands fisted on her hips, and she started talking. Troy couldn't tell what she was saying—the distance was too great and the crowd and country music were much too loud—but judging by the outrage on her face and the way her lips kept moving, Misty Sanderson was on a roll.

In less than fifteen seconds she'd wiped off Cabrerra's menacing expression; in fifteen more she had him backing up a step. When he tried to interrupt, Misty talked faster and lifted a slender finger to poke him in the chest.

Grinning, Troy picked up Smokin' Jo's and started tapping the bottle again as he enjoyed the show. If it was anyone else, he'd feel sorry for the guy. Cabrerra was starting to look embarrassed. A slash of red rose under his tanned cheeks as he glanced around and caught the broad smiles and tellingly averted faces of the men around him. His flush deepened when some of the women in the bar—less intimidated than the males by Cabrerra's scowl—started shouting encouragement to Misty.

"C'mon, honey. You tell him what's what," yelled one.

"Don't let that man get away with doin' y'all wrong," shouted another.

From the corner of his eye, Troy caught sight of the Gal's room door cautiously opening. Short Skirt peeked out—and Troy gave Smokin' Jo's an extra-hard smack.

The sauce broke loose, splattering everywhere. Cussing under his breath, Troy set the bottle down and started to mop the mess on his plate and the table with his napkin. After a couple of swipes, he abandoned the chore, and glanced around.

Short Skirt had disappeared again. Misty and Cabrerra were still going at it—at least, Misty was still talking and Cabrerra, scowl darkening, was still taking it. Misty's lips kept moving and her finger kept poking—until Cole abruptly caught her hand in one of his and put his other over her mouth.

Troy shook his head, wincing involuntarily. If Cole were to ask him—not that a Cabrerra ever would—he'd tell him that he was practically begging to get bit. As Troy had learned at a very young age, it wasn't wise to put your hand anywhere near an angry female's mouth.

Troy watched Misty's eyes narrow, then he speared a bite of sauce-drenched steak with his fork. He chewed, the spicy barbecue burning his tongue, and waited hopefully.

But before Misty could sink her small white teeth into him, Cole leaned close and whispered something in her ear. Above

Cole's palm, Misty's eyes widened, then narrowed with anger. She shoved Cole's hand away and answered him right back— and whatever she said certainly shut Cole up. In fact, he was still staring at her in dumbfounded surprise when Misty jumped off the bar stool, grabbed his wrist and her purse, and started towing him toward the door.

Cole followed her willingly. More shouted advice followed their progress, but Misty didn't pause and neither did the big man behind her. They left to the accompaniment of hoots and hollers without once looking back.

Disappointed at the outcome of the argument, Troy was staring broodingly at the swinging doors when a movement near the restroom distracted him. He glanced over as Short Skirt peered out again, then warily emerged, keeping her face averted. She headed toward her seat, her graceful walk holding Troy's un-divided interest. He smiled a little as this time she gave enough of a jump to make it up on her bar stool on her very first try. Big Bob paused in front of her to point to the door, obviously telling her where Misty had gone. Troy expected Short Skirt to leave, also, but instead, she laid her purse on the bar and reached for the beer Big Bob slid in front of her.

Troy looked around and realized he wasn't the only one watching her. Seeing her sitting alone caused a fresh ripple of interest in the room. Danny Wilson—with a casual attitude that didn't fool Troy for a second—abandoned his pool game to swagger in her direction, and ended up in Misty's abandoned seat, acting as if he'd just landed there by accident and wasn't aware of the slender blonde next to him at all. His white, chipped-tooth smile widening, Danny settled in, signaling Big Bob for a beer. It wasn't the first time Troy had seen Wilson in action. Danny worked the circuit as a rodeo clown, and in Troy's opinion, no one was better at drawing the attention of a maddened bull in the ring. Or, it seemed, a pretty woman in a bar, he mentally added, as Danny smiled at Short Skirt and she smiled back.

Time to get moving, Troy decided. Setting down his whiskey glass, he rose, then stood swaying for a few seconds, waiting for the sharp pain in his knee and the dizziness in his brain to ease. When they did, he carefully made his way to the bar—just as Dan leaned over to say something to the woman.

"Hey, Dan," Troy drawled, interrupting the other man in midsentence.

Dan glanced his way. "Troy," the cowboy replied with a distinct lack of enthusiasm.

Troy didn't take it personally. The two men were friends, but no man feels friendly to another when he's trying hard to pick up a good-looking woman, and this blonde was mouthwatering.

Troy studied her as Big Bob slid two long necks on the counter. From across the room, she'd looked attractive. Up close, she was stunning. The lashes resting against her cheeks were thick and dark, shielding her gaze as she stared at the bottles in front of her. Her cheekbones were well defined, her nose small and straight, her lips sweetly curved. But what really set her apart from most of the women Troy had met was her skin. Her glowing, sun-kissed skin was so finely textured it literally looked silky smooth. Touchable. He had to resist the urge to reach out, to run a finger along her smooth, honey-golden cheek.

As if she sensed his thought, she shifted a little, continuing to ignore him, her stiff posture as unwelcoming as Wilson's greeting had been.

Troy wasn't daunted; O'Malleys enjoyed a challenge. So he turned to Wilson. "Ready for the rodeo tomorrow?"

"Yeah."

"You planning on attending?" Troy asked, peering around the cowboy to try to catch Short Skirt's gaze.

She shrugged and turned farther away from him—a reaction that encouraged Dan to lean in closer. "You know, I didn't catch your name," Wilson said, smiling crookedly at her, "but I think I've seen you around town before. Are you a friend of Misty's from Dallas?" he asked, lowering his voice in an effort to exclude Troy.

Troy refused to be excluded. He moved, stepping blatantly between them to clap Dan on the back. "Misty's friend?" he repeated in a disbelieving tone. "Are you kidding me, Dan? Why, she was almost Misty's sister-in-law. Weren't you, Short Skirt?"

That got her. Her spine stiffened at the nickname, and she turned to meet his eyes. "Are you saying my skirt's too short?" she asked in a dangerously level tone.

"Hell, no!" Troy stared innocently into her glowering blue gaze, then at her long, long legs. He eyed them leisurely, then let his gaze travel up to her slim waist and sweet breasts—lingered there a moment—then continued higher to meet her eyes once again.

He shook his head solemnly. "No, ma'am, not at all," he replied. "In my opinion, your skirt's way too long."

Her eyes flashed; Troy repressed a grin. Damn, he loved to make her angry. He was getting ready to provoke her some more, when Dan interrupted, "What did ya mean about her being Misty's sister-in-law?" the cowboy asked uneasily, his puzzled gaze traveling from one to the other. "Do ya'll know each other?"

Reluctantly, Troy abandoned blonde-baiting to glance over at Dan. "Of course I know her, Dan. So do you. Surely you recognize Ally Cabrerra."

Chapter Four

"Uninitiated heifers can present special challenges. Often they'll spurn the male's advances and ignore all mating cues. Usually all it takes to overcome reluctance is a simple change of environment. Minimize distractions by selecting a pen large enough for the customary chase, but small enough to ensure interaction between the breeding pair...."

—*Successful Breeding: A Guide for the Cattleman*

Dan reared back like a startled stallion, the whites of his eyes showing, the stunned alarm on his face identical to the expression he'd worn at the Abilene rodeo when a bull had hooked him in the butt. "Good Lord, I'll be damned if it ain't. How're ya doin', Al—er, Ally? I'm sorry. I didn't recognize you for a minute."

"That's okay," Ally murmured, while Troy clapped him on the shoulder, saying heartily, "Now, isn't that downright amusing.

Why, when Cole returns—are your other brothers coming with him, Ally?—I'm sure they'll get a kick out of the way you were trying to hook up with their little sister, Dan, without even realizing who she was."

As a rodeo clown, Dan was accustomed to moving quickly, and Troy had to admire the speed he used to extricate himself from possible danger now. "Heck, sounds like fun," Dan said, "talking to your brothers and all," he added in clarification, the color darkening in his ruddy cheeks. "But I need to get home. Have to check my rigging before the rodeo tomorrow. See ya around, Ally. Troy." He touched the brim of his hat in farewell, then disappeared quicker than fried chicken at a church picnic, his untouched beer the sole remaining testament to his presence.

Troy took off his hat, then confiscated Dan's bar stool and stretched his bad leg out beneath the counter. He appropriated Dan's abandoned beer, as well, tilting the long neck to his lips and taking a deep, full swallow before setting the bottle down with a sigh of satisfaction.

He glanced over at Ally. She was pretending to ignore him, focusing intently on the TV perched high behind the bar as if she'd never seen a monster truck rally before. Troy drank his beer as he studied her, unable to get over how different she looked. Her drastically lightened hair framed her slim jaw in a style Misty often wore, and she'd dyed it Misty's color, too—a golden-wheat shade with stripes of platinum streaking through it. Her simple, sleeveless blouse dipped into a V displaying a modest amount of cleavage, and the rosy-red color of the garment highlighted the pink on her cheeks.

Troy finished his beer and signaled Big Bob for another. On the TV, the trucks on steroids had been replaced by a skinny kid at a flea market earnestly demonstrating the wonders of an orange chamois cloth. Big Bob muted the television volume and cranked up Jim Croce on the stereo speakers, but Ally remained focused on the now silent TV, watching as intently as if she could read the kid's lips and expected to be quizzed on the ShamWow! later.

Well, Troy had a quiz of his own to put to her, and he wanted his answers before Misty got back. So he corralled the next beer Big Bob slid toward him, then leaned in close to Ally. "So, Al. How're things going with you?" he asked, bumping her shoulder companionably with his, as if they were long-lost war buddies recently reunited.

She almost slipped off her stool. She caught herself, then answered through clenched, small white teeth without looking his way. "Things are going fine, O'Malley." Keeping her gaze fixed on the car salesman who'd replaced the ShamWow! kid, she added, "Or they would be if you'd slink on back to your hidey-hole in the corner."

"Ah, so you noticed me, did you?" Stifling a grin at the way the comment made her soft lips press together, he drawled affably, "I'll just do you that lil ole favor, as soon as you tell me what's going on, what with the change in your hair and clothes—" his gaze traveled to that nearly illegal skirt "—and all."

She turned to pin him with a cold blue glare. "And I'll just do that lil ole favor for *you*," she promised, exaggerating her drawl just as he'd done, "as soon as you tell me what concern it is of yours."

"Oh, it's not any of my concern," he responded promptly, "but curiosity is my besetting sin."

"Womanizing, drinking and lying are your besetting sins. Laziness is up there, too. Curiosity doesn't even make the list."

"And yet I'm definitely curious about all these changes." His gaze wandered over her again. "Nice ones for the most part— except for the hair."

Taken by surprise, she exclaimed, "I thought men preferred blondes!"

He shrugged. "Maybe some do. But I prefer your hair like it used to be. Long and dark. Silky-looking. Real pretty."

The sincerity in his husky tones was unmistakable. Alarmed by the bloom of pleasure she felt, Ally said caustically, "Gee, that's nice to know, O'Malley. Why don't I go outside and write that in the dirt, just in case—in some far distant future—your opinion matters to me." She snapped her fingers. "Oh, wait! I have a better idea. Why don't *you* go do it?"

If she'd hoped to deflate him, she failed miserably. Amusement danced in his green eyes. "Are you asking me to leave?"

She didn't bother mincing the matter. "Yes."

He assumed a hurt expression. "You wound me, Ally. You really do," he said sadly, then lifted his hand to regard the base of his thumb as he played the trump card he'd had on her for more than twenty years. "Again."

Ally couldn't help glancing swiftly around, guilt flickering in her chest, but she feigned ignorance. "I don't know what you're talking about."

He pretended to be surprised. "Surely you haven't forgotten *biting* me?"

His voice was loud enough to draw a start and a quick look from the man sitting on her other side. Ally glanced at the stranger, then at Troy. "No, I didn't."

Troy lifted his eyebrows. "Didn't forget or—"

"Bite you!" she said loudly.

More glances slanted their way. Trying to cover her embarrassment, Ally took a drink, mumbling into her beer bottle, "I mean, I never bit you."

"Yeah, you did, darlin'. You bit me right on the—"

"Will you hush up!" She met his gaze fiercely.

"Sure," he said agreeably. "When you own up."

Their gazes locked. Ally broke first.

"Okay," she admitted crossly, looking away, "so I bit you—"

"And left a scar."

"—and left a teeny, tiny mark—"

"Two marks."

"—at the base of your *thumb*." She emphasized the word for Big Ears by her side, whipping around so suddenly to face the eavesdropper that she caught him with his head cocked, clearly listening in. The man shifted uncomfortably under her glare, then slid off his stool and left. Ally eyed his retreating, plaid-covered back malevolently, then turned to meet Troy's gaze once more. "Big deal, so I bit you. You lived."

"Yeah, with perfect little imprints of your teeth—"

"My *baby* teeth!"

"Right there on my hand. Scars I'll bear my entire life."

She rolled her eyes. "You're a card carrying member of the Professional Bull Riders association. You likely have scars everywhere."

He nodded solemnly. "Wanna see?"

"No!"

He looked disappointed. "You sure? There's one on my hip shaped like a—"

"I don't want to know!"

"But with all the scars I have, I only have one from being bitten. By you."

Ally sipped her beer and kept her eyes on the TV, determined not to respond.

Troy sighed again, even more loudly, and rubbed his hand, shaking his head mournfully. "Man, but it sure did hurt...."

She set down her bottle with a thump. "Would you quit whining? I was three years old, for goodness' sake! You were eleven!"

"Nine."

"Plenty old enough to know better than to put your hand in a baby's mouth."

"Hey," Troy lifted his scarred hand in protest. "Kyle's the one who decided to hold the contest, not me!"

Ally grimaced. Unfortunately, that was all too true. Ally's mother Colleen had thrown a rare party for Cole's ninth birthday and Kyle—who'd been set to "baby watch" Ally—had come up with the idea of putting the time to profitable use. He'd held a contest among all Cole's little punk guests, the winner being the one who could stand his baby sister's "Ally-gator" bite the longest. And with four older brothers to practice on, Ally's bite was pretty scary.

Troy had gone first and subsequently been the winner of the impromptu event. Basically, because once she'd latched on, Ally'd stayed on, locking her little jaw tighter than a pit bull's on a juicy bone, biting him hard enough to draw blood. She'd refused to let go, until the sound of Troy's howling and all the other boys yelling had brought Colleen Cabrerra to the scene on the run. Ally had gotten her first real scolding; Kyle had gotten another of his numerous spankings; and the rest of the kids had been sent home. And Troy had been forbidden to play with those wild—and possibly rabid—Cabrerra children ever again.

Ally took a drink of beer, trying to wash the memory away. She didn't remember much from when she was a toddler, but a few distinct memories were branded on her brain. The lemony, oily smell that caught at the back of her throat whenever her mama waxed the big table inherited from Ally's grandmother. Standing at the back screen door watching her brothers outside with the dusty, metallic taste of the screen she'd licked sharp on her tongue. And, equally sharp in her mind even now was the salty, grimy taste of Troy O'Malley's hand when she'd bitten him.

The memory made her uncomfortable—*he* made her uncomfortable with those mocking, knowing eyes and his teasing, white grin. When she'd first caught sight of him sitting in his corner as she'd scurried to avoid Cole, she'd prayed he hadn't noticed her. He hadn't appeared to; his steak had seemed to have his complete attention.

And when she'd pushed open the door to the ladies' room and met her own reflection in the mirror, she'd decided it didn't matter if Troy had seen her. She'd shaken her head, watching in wonder as the slender blonde opposite did the same. How could he recognize her…when she didn't recognize herself?

Dressed in Misty's clothes, with Misty's expensive wig covering her dark hair, she looked—she even *felt*—like an entirely different person. Attractive. Confident. Sexy, even. Danny had seemed to think so, and she'd swear Theodore had given her a second look as she'd walked past him. Surreptitiously, she glanced toward the billiard tables, trying to see if he was looking at her…but she couldn't tell. Troy's wide shoulder blocked her view.

She scowled at him. He was distracting her and ruining her plan!

Troy returned her scowl with a bland smile and finished off his beer. Setting his empty bottle with a sigh of regret, he picked up his hat. "Well, little darlin'," he said as he put it on and slid off his bar stool, "it's been fun, but I'd better get a move on…"

Good!

"Now, don't you try to stop me…"

Like that would happen. Ally rolled her eyes.

"…I need to talk to Buck Boulter about picking up that lease offer you declined."

He took a limping step away—and Ally grabbed him. "Wait a minute!"

Troy pulled up short. His gaze fastened on her fingers, digging into his muscled forearm.

Horrified by the jolt of sexual awareness tingling through her fingers, Ally hurriedly released him. His gaze rose to meet hers.

Flushing under his enigmatic stare, Ally swallowed and forced out, "Please."

His eyebrows lifted. Troy eased onto his bar stool, his gaze sharpening on her face. "Now, this is interesting," he drawled. "A few minutes ago you were all-fired hot to get rid of me."

"Yes, well, it's just…" Ally fiddled with her purse, put it in her lap, then set it on the bar. She picked up her beer bottle, then lowered it again, carefully aligning the bottom to cover a wet ring on the wood. "About that lease…"

"The one you turned down."

"The one Cole turned down."

Troy shrugged. "Same thing."

"No, it isn't." She looked up from her task and met his gaze straight on. "My aunt left that land *to me*—" she took a deep breath "—and I'm willing to accept your offer to lease Bride's Price. For the amount you offered."

Troy's brow creased in puzzlement. "It doesn't matter. Your brother will never allow it."

"He won't have a choice in the matter."

"But Cole controls the land until—" Troy's eyes widened. He stared at the determined expression on her face, then gave a long, low whistle. "Holy hell, that's what this is all about. Your hair, new clothes. Why you hid in the ladies' room when Cole came in—hell, why you're here in Big Bob's in the first place. You're planning on roping some poor cowboy into marriage!"

At any other time, on any other subject, his dumbfounded expression would have filled Ally with satisfaction. After all, it wasn't every day you could surprise Troy O'Malley. But right now—on this particular subject—his expression ticked her off. Big time. "It's not like that at all."

"Sure it's not," he said, his disbelieving expression never changing. He shook his head a little as if to clear it, then looked around the bar. "So who is it?" he asked, his square jaw tightening slightly. "Who's the poor dude you're planning on conning into a proposal?"

"I'm not planning on *conning* anyone."

He ignored that, turning his head to study her face speculatively, his eyes narrowing. "I haven't heard that you're dating anyone special. Or even," he added after a moment's consideration, "anyone not so special."

Ally clenched her teeth. "I'm not. But that doesn't mean—" She hated beer, but she was going on her second bottle, anyway, so she took another sip to bolster her nerve. "That doesn't mean I can't get someone to willingly marry me."

"No, ma'am. I mean, yes, ma'am, of course you can. I'm sure there are *thousands* of men who want you."

A couple cowboys looked their way. Ally hunched her shoulders. "Would you lower your voice!" she hissed.

"Oops, sorry." Hitching his bar stool closer, Troy hunched his broad shoulders, too, and pulled his hat lower before glancing around furtively—just like an inept spy in an old movie, she thought irritably. He even spoke out of the corner of his mouth as he asked, "So who are you planning to trap—ask?"

"Like I'm going to tell *you*," she responded witheringly.

"Hey! I want to help."

"Yeah, right." She sipped her beer, trying to ignore him again.

He ignored her ignoring. "Not Dan," he decided. "You let him slip away too easily. Now, who...?" He surveyed the room again, frowning thoughtfully and finally focused on a nearby table. "It's Red, isn't it? Every woman's dream man."

Ally glanced at Red Ruppelt, who'd laid his head amidst his collection of liquor glasses and ash trays to take a refreshing snooze. Drool trickled down his bristly red beard, pooling on his table. More like every woman's nightmare. "Uck."

"Not Red then? How 'bout Clancy McGee? A true Texas icon, who even looks willing."

Ally peeked in Clancy's direction. He looked willing, all right. When she inadvertently met his gaze, the old cowboy lifted his mug in a silent salute and gave her a wide, toothless grin. She smiled politely, but quickly returned her attention to her bottle. When Misty said men would come out of the woodwork, Ally hadn't realized she meant it literally. "Yeah, right."

"You'd better tell me, then," Troy warned. "So I can move away. If I stay here, chances are your prospective groom will think we're together and won't come over."

"No one could ever believe that." Still, she snuck a glance at the pool table to make sure.

"Damn!" Troy had followed her gaze, and was staring toward the men playing pool, too. "So that's who it is!" He shook his head doubtfully. "I don't know, Ally. He sure looks pissed about my sitting here. Don't look now—"

She looked, anyway. "No, he's not!" she said, watching Theodore briskly hit a ball into a corner pocket. "He hasn't even noticed you!" She glanced at Troy indignantly—and met his knowing, mocking eyes straight on.

Her mouth snapped shut.

"Theodore Bayor," Troy said softly. Something flickered in his slitted gaze—anger? disapproval?—that made Ally uneasy. But before she could decide what it was, he blinked and the expression disappeared, replaced by a bland look. "Who would've thunk it?" he asked.

Ally resisted the urge to whack his head with her bottle. "Go away, O'Malley," she said again.

He shook his head, and his expression turned reproving. "I

would," he said, "but I really want to lease that land from you. And although I'm happier than a pig in a puddle to know you're trying to make that possible, I'm sorry, Al, but it appears you're going to need some help here."

"I don't—"

"You're not seriously planning to pursue a married man, are you?" he interrupted her.

Ally's eyes widened in shock. "Theodore Bayor isn't married!"

"Oh, no? Who do you think Mrs. Bayor is?"

Ally started off strong. "She's Theodore's—" but finished on a doubtful note "—mother?"

Troy shook his brown head reprovingly. "Now, who on earth told you that?"

"Misty thought…Tammy told her…" Ally frowned, trying to remember exactly what had been said. "I guess we just assumed, because she's so much older than he is, that Mrs. Bayor had to be his mother," she said unhappily, adding in her own defense, "why, she looks like she's at least seventy!"

"Ally, Ally, Ally," Troy said chidingly. "How prejudiced can you be? A lot of older women are marrying younger men now."

"It's not only that!" Ally thought of the woman's broad, scowling face as she'd glared through the window; the dark dress she'd been wearing on a hot Texas day. "She seems so…grumpy. And dresses so old-fashioned."

"When it comes to true love," Troy said piously, "it's what's inside that counts."

Ally slanted him a sidelong glance. He was right, of course; she certainly couldn't argue with that sentiment. She admitted, "They *are* from California."

"Ah, cougar country." Troy nodded wisely. "No surprise there. They probably lived in Orange County."

"Maybe. I just didn't think…" Ally shook her head in lingering bewilderment. No wonder Troy had given her such a strange look before. How could she have jumped to such an erroneous conclusion? "I'm so embarrassed."

Troy slipped his arm around her shoulders to give her a comforting squeeze. "That's okay. We all make mistakes. Even me."

"Yes, but— Oh, what am I doing here?" How had she lived in this town her entire life, and not noticed the dearth of eligible men? This was cowboy country, for goodness' sake. Yet every man around was either married, old, creepy or related to her.

Ally shoved her bottle across the counter and grabbed her red purse. "I'm getting out of here. This whole idea is stupid."

She started to climb from her stool, but the comforting arm around her shoulders suddenly clamped tight, holding her in place. "Whoa! Wait a minute!" Troy said. "Just because you put your money on a lame gelding in the first race, doesn't mean you can't recover in the second. Your idea isn't stupid. In fact, I think I can help you, if you just—" He broke off to glance around. "It's too crowded in here to talk. C'mon outside. We'll take a walk and sort through this."

Without giving her time to protest, he grasped her waist and lifted her off the stool. As soon as her feet hit the floor, he curved his hand around her elbow and led her—willy-nilly—from the bar.

Several pairs of eyes tracked their progress to the exit. Ally didn't seem to notice, but Troy met the male glances slanted their way with a challenging stare. And when he caught Bayor, standing by the billiard table with his cue resting on the floor, staring at Ally, too, Troy's scowl darkened. It annoyed him that Ally had considered asking Bayor—brand-new to Tangleweed and a virtual stranger to all intents and purposes—to aid in her scheme. So he put a little extra menace in his expression when he caught Bayor's eyes, causing the other man to redirect his attention to the pool table where it belonged.

Outside, Troy scanned the parking lot. "Misty's car is gone," he pointed out. "Cole's pickup is still here, though."

Ally didn't comment on that, so he added, "He must have left with Misty."

"Maybe" was all Ally replied, giving him a considering look. She made an observation of her own. "Dan's truck is gone, too. Guess he did go home."

Troy didn't doubt it. Dan had definitely turned green at the thought of arousing the Cabrerra brothers' ire.

Ally started walking along the scraggly path leading to the arena in the distance, and Troy fell into step at her side, grasping her arm when she stumbled on a tuft of rank grass. She gave him a sidelong glance, but didn't pull away from his hold, seemingly too preoccupied with her own thoughts—or maybe a little tipsy from her beers. Troy was certainly feeling no pain. His knee wasn't hurting at all.

They'd only gone a short way when she said slowly, "Dan really didn't recognize me, did he? He looked at me like he'd never seen me before. Isn't that strange?"

"Yeah," Troy agreed. But he didn't really mean it; he understood exactly how Dan had felt. Troy had known Ally all his life, too. She'd always been "one of those Cabrerras"—the tagalong little sister who'd bitten his hand as a big-eyed toddler, and who—all grown up—gave him disdainful looks whenever their gazes happened to meet.

But then, at last year's rodeo, he'd looked at Ally and seen her—*really* seen her—for the very first time.

He'd been standing near the judges' stand, idly watching the Cabrerras, thinking it must be nice to have brothers always watching your back, and a little sister to admire you, cheer you on when you rode. He glanced at the sister. She'd appeared pensive as she strode along, her gaze fixed on the dusty ground, the Cabrerra men surrounding her as they most always did in a crowd—the way cattle'll surround a newborn calf when predators threaten. She hadn't noticed the cowboys swaggering past to check her out, and she hadn't noticed Troy as he stared, unwillingly transfixed by the sight of her long, slender, golden legs in her cutoff jeans shorts.

Then, as if she'd felt his eyes on her, she'd suddenly looked up, her solemn blue gaze locking with his. And Troy discovered that hormones were pesky little things. They could race from a man's groin up to his brain in a half second flat, scrambling his thinking entirely. Tricking him into believing a slim, small-breasted female in a simple white T-shirt and shorts—a Cabrerra female, at that!—was the sexiest thing he'd ever laid eyes on.

So he'd winked at her—and she'd blinked. She lifted her chin and walked away with the rest of the Cabrerra herd. But the faint contempt in her blue eyes had pricked him that day like it never had before. As if a prickly pear burr he'd brushed off before had suddenly gotten under his skin, burrowing deep. He'd wanted to irritate her—make her notice him—the way he did her.

So after his ride—a damn good one—he'd sauntered over to where she stood watching by the rails. "Taking notes for your brother?" he asked, still dusting off his Wranglers.

"Yeah," she'd drawled sweetly. "On how not to be a conceited show-off."

Troy nodded solemnly. "Kyle definitely needs help with that."

Her blue eyes narrowed, and she stomped away, not even waiting to watch her brother—the next one out of the chute—ride his bull. And ever since then Troy'd watch for her, waiting for the chance to send her a needling look or make a teasing remark to rile her.

Sometimes he got the best of those brief, usually wordless encounters; sometimes she did. Like in Mesquite, when he'd drawn a bull that spun faster and kicked higher than a Vegas showgirl on speed. He'd ended up landing on his new "Boss of the Plains" Stetson, flattening it completely, and even as he sprinted toward the fence, squished hat in hand, he'd seen Ally in the bleachers, laughing so hard she was bent at the waist, arms wrapped around her stomach.

He'd had to fight the desire to go to her. To grab her and kiss her and make her stop. Someday, he'd promised himself. Someday he'd kiss all the sass right out of her.

But he'd never gotten the chance. Because soon after that, Misty's engagement broke up, and the lifelong rivalry between Troy and the Cabrerra brothers had gone from earnest to downright ugly, especially with Cole. And Ally—until their brief exchange at her great-aunt's funeral—not only wouldn't talk to him, but had taken to ignoring him completely whenever they ran into each other. Like she'd first tried to do tonight.

But she couldn't ignore him now, he thought with satisfaction, looking down at her, savoring the smoothness of her cool skin beneath his callused hand. Not if she wanted that lease. Not when they were alone together, out in the quiet Texas night, with no one else around.

Troy remained silent, letting the warm darkness wrap around them as they walked along. The noise from Big Bob's had dimmed immediately upon leaving the bar, and by the time they reached the arena, could barely be heard at all above the night sounds of the prairie. The rough stock, brought in by the contractor for the next day's festivities, were standing easy in the pens near the rodeo grounds, mumbling to one another with snorts and soft grunts, with the occasional mournful bellow splitting the dark. Troy half expected Ally to keep going in that direction, to check out the bulls and broncs, but instead she broke away to wander over to the main arena. Resting her arms on a middle board, she peered through the rails at the empty show ring.

Troy followed and leaned his shoulder against an upper rail, standing close enough to feel the warmth of her slender body against his side and to catch a sweet whiff of the perfume she wore, rising above the scents of sage and sawdust. He recognized it as Misty's perfume. It smelled fine on Misty—on Ally, it assumed a deeper, richer note. Became pure enticement. Made his head spin.

Trying to clear his mind, he looked around. It wasn't much of a facility. In daylight, the place looked even more pitiful than it did under the big old yellow Texas moon hanging in the sky. He knew from experience that the ancient speakers flanking the judges' stand sounded tinny, and that the red paint was cracked and peeling on the billboard that declared Welcome to Tangleweed, Texas. Our Roots Run Deep. Now the moonlight leached the faded colors from the rickety bleachers and beat-up chutes, coating everything in soothing shades of charcoal. The sawdust looked velvety soft, and a small, black mound of earth just inside the fence marked where a not-too-smart prairie dog was trying to start a new colony.

The little critter popped up from its hole suddenly, sitting on its haunches to eye Troy curiously, then clasped its front paws together in a pleading gesture, its tiny jaw moving frantically as if offering urgent advice.

Troy glanced at Ally. She hadn't noticed the rodent but was staring off into the distance, her chin resting on her arms, still lost in thought.

Shifting to relieve the pain pinging in his knee, he studied her. Damn, she was pretty—even with that blond hair that he just couldn't get used to on her. In the moonlight, her golden skin looked pearly white. Against the pale gleam of her face, just beneath the fringe of hair on her forehead, her dark eyebrows curved in delicate, black lines above her long-lashed, shadowy eyes. Her nose was small and straight. Her wide lips were pursed in thought, forming a plump pucker.

Troy swallowed. He wanted to touch those inviting lips with his thumb. To gently tug the full bottom, open her up. Taste her—

She looked up. His breath caught as her big eyes, framed by the dark fan of her lashes and gleaming in the moonlight, met his. His gaze dropped back to her mouth. He started to lean down, his eyes drifting shut—

"I still can't believe that Theodore is married."

Troy's eyes shot open and he straightened abruptly. He released his breath with an exasperated hiss that caused the little prairie dog to duck back into its hole.

Was that what she'd been thinking about all this time? Theodore Bayor? "Forget about him," he told her.

"I can't. I really thought he'd be perfect."

"Well, he's not," Troy said curtly.

She didn't agree, but at least she didn't argue, which Troy decided to take as a positive. Dropping her arms from the fence, she straightened, then stretched a little. Sticking her hands in the back pockets of her skirt, she commented, "Pretty beat-up, isn't it?"

"Yeah."

"I'm surprised your grandfather hasn't put money in this place. He's certainly got his hand in every other business in Tangleweed."

A slightly acid note in her voice told Troy how she felt about that. But he shrugged, refusing to be baited—or goaded into telling her that he, and not his grandfather, was the one investing in the town. In the motel, in Big Bob's, in a couple of other places, as well.

He rested an arm against an upper rail and propped his boot against a lower. "He's not interested in rodeos."

"And he doesn't like you participating." Her tone made it a statement, not a question. "So why do you?"

"Same reason, I suppose, that your brother does."

"Kyle needs the money," Ally said bluntly. "You don't."

Troy looked out over the empty arena again. No, he didn't need the money. And she was right about his grandfather not liking him participating. Bull riding, Old Mick had declared more than once, was a sport where one dumb animal rode another in an effort to get killed.

But Troy wasn't looking to get killed when he rode—just the opposite. From the moment he climbed down onto the broad, bony back of the animal in the chute, until he landed on his feet or his face in the dust of the arena, time stood still. The gnawing, empty restlessness that increasingly plagued him completely disappeared. Never did he feel so totally calm, yet so totally alive, as he did when riding a churning, bucking bull.

"I enjoy winning," he said lightly. *And winning was especially sweet,* he added silently to himself, *when he beat a Cabrerra.* "This is the year I plan to take first in the National finals."

She gave him a wry look. "I imagine every pro rider has that plan," she said dryly. "I know Kyle does."

"Yeah, but Kyle's below me in the rankings." Not much below, but still below.

"That's true," she acknowledged, her tone thoughtful. "But Kyle has moved up six slots over the past year, while you've moved down—what is it? Three? Four?"

She knew damn well it was five, Troy thought, his gaze narrowing on her oh-so-innocent expression. Not that he'd give her the satisfaction of admitting it.

She prodded him again. "And hasn't your average gone down, too? To what? Eighty-five?"

Eighty-four. Okay, if she was trying to push his buttons, prick his pride…she was succeeding.

So he returned fire by giving her a slow, satisfied smile as he lifted his brows inquiringly. "Been tracking my stats, have you? Isn't that a sign of a crush?"

She smiled with false sweetness. "I wouldn't know. But since Kyle is the one who did the tracking—and just happened to mention he was gaining on you—I tend to doubt it."

Yeah, so did Troy. Thank God. Before he could launch another salvo, Ally got in a zing of her own. "But I have been wondering one thing about you…." She tapped a long, slender finger thoughtfully against her soft pink lips.

Troy couldn't look away from that finger, those lips. "Yeah?" he said absently.

"Aren't you getting a little old to ride bulls?"

He straightened, his boot dropping from the rails to the ground. Okay, now she was stepping over the line—going from mildly annoying to downright mean. Yeah, he was getting older; Troy knew that. He'd been rodeoing since he was a kid. At twenty he'd get bucked off ten times in a row and never feel a thing. Now, at thirty, every time he bit the dust he got up hurting. But the point was, he still got up—in every way that mattered.

"I figure I've still got a few rides in me. After all," he drawled, "Kyle's only a couple years younger than I am, and I don't suppose he's planning to quit."

"No, he's not," she admitted.

She seemed to sigh…and Troy frowned. "I thought you liked rodeos. Didn't you used to barrel race?"

Ally nodded reluctantly. "Yeah. I even did some trick riding for a while, until I was about fourteen."

"Why did you quit?"

"My horse died."

Troy felt bad. Teasing her was one thing; touching a wound quite another. "That's tough."

"Yeah, well, Pepper was pretty old. She originally belonged

to my mother. I could have trained another one, but I just never seemed to have the time."

"What kept you so busy?"

"School and stuff. Helping out at home. Sports. One of the few benefits of growing up with big brothers is that I was pretty good at sports—swimming, gymnastics."

"Oh, yeah? I took gymnastics in school, too."

Ally nodded, apparently unimpressed. "Yeah, so did Kyle. For balance. He was even offered a scholarship, but accepted one for bull riding instead at Texas A&E"

Troy had ridden for the Longhorns himself.

"Did you go to college?" he asked Ally.

She shook her head. "No, I wanted to work with horses and make money as quickly as possible. So I got certified as a farrier."

"You're a farrier?" Troy was surprised. "I didn't know that. At the Running M, we've always used Lewis Smith."

"Everyone in the county uses Smith," Ally said dryly. "Except us, of course."

Troy started to pursue the subject, when the sounds of doors slamming and motors roaring to life outside the bar distracted him. Some of the patrons would be heading on home, but he could see a large group of cowboys walking toward the arena, probably planning to bed down beneath the bleachers or in an empty pen in preparation for the rodeo the next day.

He looked at Ally. They still hadn't talked seriously about her *plan*. "We'd better be getting back. We've got a few things to settle before you head on home," he drawled a bit grimly, taking her elbow.

She let him hold her arm as they walked in silence, according the cowboys a brief nod as they passed. It wasn't until they were almost to the bar that she spoke, asking, "Why are you limping?"

"Blister."

She shot him a skeptical look. "I saw you limping at the funeral, too."

"It's a pretty bad one," he replied, lying easily. When they reached Big Bob's gravel lot, they skirted the bar to head down the darkened Main Street.

She checked abruptly, digging her heels into the boardwalk and pulling loose from his hold. "If you're heading to the diner, that'll be closing, too," she told him.

"I thought we'd talk in my motel room."

"You have a motel room?" Her big eyes narrowed.

"Yeah. I get one when the rodeo is in town, so if I stay out drinking—"

"If?"

"—I can get plenty of sleep and still make my event on time," he finished, ignoring her interruption. And, as a silent part-owner of the place, he had a room at his disposal whenever it was needed.

Still, since her frown hadn't eased, he added with a shrug, "Or—if you're nervous about going to my room—we can sit in your brother's truck or mine to discuss everything. But we might get interrupted—" he paused "—when Cole comes back."

He wasn't sure if it was the mention of her brother or the comment about her uneasiness that caused it, but she changed her mind.

"I'm not nervous. Your motel room is fine," she said. But she didn't look too happy about her decision.

The motel wasn't far, and like everything else in "downtown" Tangleweed, the pink-stuccoed building was faded and worn. Troy didn't care about that; the No-Tell-Motel—as the locals called it—was clean enough and located conveniently close to Big Bob's bar as well as the rodeo grounds.

But the lady by his side was apparently pickier about where she spent her nights. She hesitated before trailing him beneath the high wooden arch that proclaimed "Western Paradise," and her steps slowed even more as they made their way down the narrow, pink-tiled walkway to the brown door marked with a "9" that had tumbled over into a crooked number 6.

Troy glanced down at Ally as he fit his key into the lock. The bare bulb next to the door clearly illuminated her face. The distaste indicated by the slight wrinkling of her small nose, the wariness in her stance, told him art deco meets the Old West was definitely not her thing.

Sure enough, once he got the door opened, she balked. "Why don't we just talk out here."

"We can sit down inside."

"I'm not sure this is such a good idea…."

"Sure it is," Troy assured her, keeping his tone easy as he stepped closer. She stood firm as he crowded her, but when he put his hand on her lower back to encourage her inside, she bolted over the threshold like a nervous filly jumping forward at the touch of a spur. She came to a dead stop in the middle of the room and stood there, eyeing the bed, but before she could protest again, he said, "Excuse me a second," and limped to the small lamp on the nightstand. He switched it on. He reached for the duffel bag he'd slung on the bed and, zipping it open, pawed through his shaving supplies and condoms until he found the small plastic bottle of painkillers the doctor had prescribed. Twisting the cap off, he shook a couple pills into his hand and downed them with one swallow.

"What are those?"

He almost jumped, her voice was so close. Eyebrows rising in surprise, he swung around to face her. She stood almost at his elbow, trying to see the bottle in his hand. He closed his fingers around it, hiding it from her view. "Just aspirin," he drawled, torn between amusement and irritation at the disapproval on her face.

She lifted her eyebrows and glanced up at him. "For a blister?"

"Yeah." Her eyebrows lifted higher, and he admitted grudgingly, "And my knee. It's a bit sore."

He thought he saw concern flash in her eyes, before exasperation crossed her face. "I knew something was wrong. Did you sprain it?"

"Nah, like I said, it's just a little sore. Not really hurting at all."

"I see." She might as well have said "liar, liar, pants on fire," her tone was so skeptical. "If it's hurting, maybe you shouldn't compete tomorrow."

"Are you kidding?" He was honestly dumbfounded by the suggestion. "Do you think I want my standings to go down even more? If I can walk, I can ride a bull. Hell, if someone gets me on it beforehand and picks me up out of the dirt afterward, I don't even need to walk." He shook his head. "There's no way I'd ever withdraw."

She gave a faint shrug. "Well, it's none of my business, but you might want to at least sit down and take off your boot before your leg stiffens so much you can't."

She was right. Grudgingly, Troy sat on the desk chair and heeled off one boot, then the other. "Are you happy now?" he asked dryly—as if doing her a favor.

"Ecstatic."

He couldn't help smiling a little. He set his boots aside, then rose, testing his knee. "Great. So, about that lease. I want to get that herd settled in as soon as possible."

Ally seemed to brace herself. "I know you think my idea is stupid, but if you can just wait a week or so, until I can find someone to help me out—"

"Whoa, there," Troy said. "I don't think your idea is stupid—just your choice of prospective, ah, business partners. Especially when there's someone who's so perfect for the job, that I can't believe you haven't thought of him already."

"Oh, yeah? Who's that?"

"Me."

For a split second, Ally didn't move as she processed the absurdity of his comment. Then, "I'm outta here," she muttered, and sprinted for the door.

Somehow, Troy managed to cut in front of her. Maybe he could move faster without his boots, Ally thought. In any event, he beat her there and blocked the door with his body. "Wait a minute—"

"Move!"

"There's no need to get all riled up." Leaning his shoulders back against the door frame, he gave her a reproachful look. "C'mon, Ally. Hear me out. I'm just trying to help you. Help both of us."

"Yeah, right."

He lifted his hands, palms facing outward, like the innocent victim of a holdup. "You're the one who came up with the initial plan, after all." He paused, then added, "And I feel kind of bad spoiling it for you. Letting you know about Theodore Bayor and all."

Ally, still watching him warily, relaxed a little. He hadn't had to warn her, after all, that Theodore was married. He could have let her make a fool of herself. "You don't have to feel bad," she said grudgingly. "I appreciate you letting me know that Theodore is married."

"No problem. And you know it makes sense—you, me— teaming up. We both want me to lease the land. If we work together, that can happen. Hell, chances are, we won't even have to go through with the dastardly deed. Most likely, just the threat of us getting married will make your brother change his mind."

She wanted to believe it; it was the same argument she'd made to Misty. But remembering the hatred on Cole's face when he looked at Troy—as well as the glint in Troy's eye as he'd returned her brother's stare—she just didn't think it would work. "My brothers would kill you," she said with absolute conviction.

In the blink of an eye, Troy's good ole boy facade disappeared. His jaw tightened and his green eyes turned hard. "There're a lot of things you can believe about me, but there's one thing you can bank on. I'm not afraid of your brothers. The big question here is—" he pointed a long finger in her direction "—are you?"

"Me?" She shook her head. "Of course not."

"Then, I don't see the problem."

"Then, you've landed on your head too many times riding bulls. My brothers aside, no one is going to believe that you— that I—that you and I could ever be attracted to each other."

"Yeah, they will. If we make it believable enough."

"And how're we going to do that?"

"Like this."

Reaching out, he caught her in his arms.

And he kissed her.

Chapter Five

"Make sure the breeding ground is flat and free of obstruction. Warning to the reader: If the bull has to struggle for balance, injury may result."
—*Successful Breeding: A Guide for the Cattleman*

Caught unprepared, Ally wanted to argue. But with Troy's lips pressed to hers, all she could manage was "Mmmph?"

Alarmed by her racing pulse, she lifted her hands to push him away…then hesitated as his warm, dry lips rasped gently across hers. She remained still, fingers splayed against his broad chest, as he repeated the caress, brushing his mouth back and forth over hers, again and again. Bemused, her eyes drifted shut.

Although her experience was limited, she still had enough to recognize an expert when she met one lip to lip. And Troy O'Malley was definitely a master. The subtle, sweet friction of his mouth on hers made her lips tingle—become oh, so sensitive. Made her nipples tighten and her fingers curl against his chest to clutch at his shirt. When he used the hot, damp tip of his tongue to delicately trace the seam of her swollen lips, desire lanced through her. She moaned and clutched his shirt tighter, murmuring softly against his lips.

Troy lifted his head. Bereft at the loss of his mouth, Ally forced her eyes open.

His eyes were dark and heavy-lidded. His face—half shadowed, half illuminated by the light of the small lamp—wore a taut, hungry expression that made her stomach swoop with excitement.

She tensed in his hold and his arms tightened. His intent gaze moved over her face, then he lowered his head to press his rough cheek against her soft one, drawling huskily, "What did you say?"

His warm breath tickled her ear, making her shiver. She swallowed heavily, trying to speak. "I said I feel…kind of dizzy."

"Yeah? Me, too." He waited. Nuzzled her cheek. "Do you wanna stop?"

Ally didn't know; she wasn't sure. The sage-tinted night air that still clung to his clothes, the feel of his warm skin, the look in his hungry eyes—all distracted her, blurring her thoughts. She shook her head to clear it…and immediately his lips settled on hers again, this time nudging hers compellingly, urging them to part. Helplessly, she complied, and he slanted his mouth to deepen the kiss. His demanding tongue slipped in to claim hers, stealing her breath and the last of her willpower. Making her mind spin until the only thought left was *Troy Michael O'Malley is one hell of a kisser.*

Then even that thought floated away as Ally became lost in sensation—the sweet whiskey taste of his mouth, the enticing heat of his hard body. Releasing his shirt, she struggled to free her arms, then looped them around his strong neck. Leaning against him, she returned the caress of his tongue with hers and the hard arm banding her waist cinched tighter in response. His belt buckle jabbed against her midriff; the more beguiling hardness beneath it pressed lower. She cuddled against him, trying to get closer.

Troy helped by widening his stance to fit her soft curves snugly against him as he continued to kiss her. Without lifting his mouth, he slid one hand smoothly down the front of her blouse, deftly undoing buttons, then pushed it aside to find the front clasp of her bra. Two seconds later he'd snapped it open.

Ally gasped and stiffened in his embrace, her arms lowering to try to brace against his chest.

"Shh, shh, it's okay," Troy murmured, and began kissing her again—slow deep kisses that made her soften in his arms…and made him harden against her with increasing urgency.

But he didn't rush her. He kept his movements slow and easy, not touching her breasts, just waiting until she'd melted against him once again before he began to lazily stroke her back through her silky shirt, his palm roaming over her delicate shoulder blades and down the long, straight line of her spine.

Ally shivered at the caress, and he stroked her again, a long, tender caress that she hazily realized was gliding toward her hair. Reaching out blindly, she pushed his arm downward, not wanting him to touch Misty's wig.

But Troy obviously mistook her intention, interpreting her gesture to mean she wanted his touch elsewhere. He slid both his hands down her thighs, then up under her skirt to cup the firm cheeks of her bottom in his callused palms.

Ally gasped into his mouth, and he moaned into hers, suddenly lifting her off her feet.

Her sandals fell to the floor, and her arms tightened around his neck. Instinctively, Ally wrapped her legs around his hips for safety as he lifted her higher to kiss her again—those long, drugging kisses that stole her breath and clouded her brain, kisses that made her strain against him in mindless need. She burrowed her hands in his thick hair, sifting through it, letting the short, coarse curls slide between her fingers. Kissing him back as deeply as he was kissing her.

Troy groaned—then groaned again, staggering. He bumped into the nightstand, knocking the lamp to the floor where it lay on its side, lighting a dim path across the dusty wood floor.

"Damn leg," Troy muttered, turning toward the bed. He intended to gently lower Ally to the mattress, but his knee gave out. He stumbled, hit the box spring and lost his balance. He dropped her—then crashed on top of her, crushing her into the mattress.

Ally gasped, and Troy reared up, lifting his chest off her. "Are you okay?"

"My ribs… Your elbow caught them."

"I'm sorry, darlin'." He covered her fingers with his over the sore spot, pushing her hand aside to gently rub away the pain himself. He began kissing her again, quick comforting kisses on her smooth cheek and silky temple as he muttered huskily, "Damn elbow."

She half smiled, then winced, and he asked gently, "Still hurting?"

She shook her head and shifted awkwardly beneath him. "It's your buckle. Jabbing me."

"Ah…" He moved off her completely and sat up on the side of the bed. Ally drew a deep breath of relief and rubbed her sore ribs, staring up at the cracked plaster ceiling, thinking that she should sit up, too. A movement from Troy drew her attention, and she lazily looked over as he yanked his shirt off and tossed it aside. Distracted by the ripple of muscles in his broad back, she didn't quite realize he was undressing completely until he stood up, swaying a little, to unfasten his belt and Wranglers. Then he shucked them—briefs and all—right to the floor.

Eyes rounding, she blinked in hazy surprise at his tight, masculine butt—*hey, he did have a scar, shaped like a steer head*—but before she could move or say anything, he lay down beside her, taking her in his arms again, asking huskily, "That better, honey?"

Ally could barely hear, much less answer his question as his hand slid beneath her panties, and slipped them down. Her blouse and bra were already undone, and her skirt had bunched around her waist. As she assimilated the fact that she was lying—practically naked—in Troy O'Malley's bed, he rolled on top of her. His hips nestled intimately between her thighs, and okay, maybe he was right, she thought dreamily. The smooth skin of his muscular shoulders and back did feel better than his shirt beneath her stroking hands. His hair-roughened chest against her breasts felt better, too, and she moaned with pleasure.

Entranced by the soft sound, Troy bent his head to kiss her again. He drew on her quivering mouth, shuddering with the hot pleasure of making love to Ally. Of tasting her sweet, sassy mouth, and feeling her slender, slightly callused fingertips tenderly stroking his scalp and nape. Of feeling her bare breasts against his chest, her silky soft thighs against his.

He wanted to see her—taste all of her honey-gold skin. With a groan, he lifted his head—and it swam with the movement. Man, she was right about feeling dizzy, he decided. He kept feeling it, too. Dizzy and…light-headed. As if his mind was floating—a weird contrast to the heaviness in his loins, hot and thickened by arousal. His lower body grew heavier still as his blurring gaze drifted over her, his muscles tightening at the sight of the smooth, golden skin of her slim neck and shoulders.

The tender curves of her breasts were half hidden by her blouse, and he lifted his hand to brush it back. But his hand wouldn't lift. And the heaviness was spreading, anchoring his arms and legs to the mattress as his mind drifted farther and farther away.

He felt her move beneath him, shifting to brace her slender hands against his shoulders. He looked into her eyes—she had such big eyes. As big and blue and wide as the Texas sky…

He blinked at her, then his eyes fell shut. He laid his head on her soft breasts to rest a moment. He could feel her heart, beating rapidly beneath his cheek. As if from a great distance, he heard her ask uncertainly, "Troy? Are you okay?"

Fighting the overwhelming lassitude, he opened his eyes again. He should have fixed the lamp. The room was growing darker, dimming around the edges. But he didn't need to see; he could feel her, writhing beneath him, her hands pushing at his shoulders. Urging him on.

With an immense effort he surged forward. His hips slid against her soft thighs. The gray darkness exploded into a million tiny stars….

Then turned black.

Pregnancy tests. Standing in an Austin drugstore three weeks later, Ally decided there had to be a million of them.

Okay, maybe not a million—but way more than she'd expected. More expensive than she'd expected, too, ranging in price from twelve dollars all the way to thirty. Which made it just that much harder to decide which one to choose.

She pulled a pink cellophane-wrapped box off the shelf. *A ninety-nine-percent accuracy rate,* it promised on the side. She put it back and checked other brands, trying to find one that guaranteed complete accuracy. None did. Then there apparently was the problem of reading the little sticks. Some gave results in lines; others in dots. One promised to actually spell it out: Pregnant or Not Pregnant. That made sense. She grabbed it along with four others of varying types and prices and carried them to the checkout counter.

The clerk standing by the register had red hair, looked sixteen, and wore a badge that read, Hi, I'm Lisa! Customer Satisfaction Is My Goal! Lisa's purple eye shadow matched her nail polish and the big wad of grape bubble gum in her mouth. Ally was ninety-nine-percent positive she'd never seen Lisa before in her life. Which was precisely why she'd made the two-hour drive into Austin instead of buying a test in Tangleweed: so she'd get a clerk she didn't know and who didn't know her.

Lisa blew a big purple bubble and popped it noisily as she reached for the first box.

Ally slapped a hand on top of it to stop her. "Just a minute. I'm buying these for a friend. Can you tell me which one is the best?"

Lisa stared at her blankly, snapped her gum and then sighed. She looked down, pawed disinterestedly through the pile, then announced in a bored tone, "They're pretty much the same, I guess."

"Well, she wanted me to get a backup. And a backup to the backup. But can I return them? If she doesn't use them all, I mean?" Ally elaborated in response to Lisa's *ya-gotta-be-kidding-me* expression.

Lisa's expression didn't change. "I dunno. No one's ever tried to before."

Ally heard someone walking up behind her, but she ignored the other customer along with the impatient clicking of Lisa's purple nails on the counter. No way, Ally decided, was she going to make the same mistake she'd made with her bridesmaid dress and buy something she couldn't return. "Can you please find out?"

Lisa gave a long-suffering sigh. Gathering up the boxes, she wandered off, presumably in search of the person in charge.

Ally watched her desultory progress for a few seconds and stifled her own sigh. It appeared Lisa would be a while. She turned to apologize for the delay to the other customer—and gasped at the heavy-browed visage behind her. "Mrs. Bayor!"

The woman's brows—make that unibrow; the two had become one—rose in surprise. "Do I know you?"

"Ah, no. But I live in Tangleweed, and I—" Ally faltered as the woman's thin lips curved down in a frown, and the unibrow began lowering ominously "—I've seen you in your store."

The unibrow made its final descent, landing directly over a pair of accusing brown eyes. "I do remember you!" Mrs. Bayor declared. "You're one of those women who was stalking my son, Theodore!"

"Your son!" Ally gaped at her all over again. "I thought he was your husband!"

"What?" Looking half flattered, half affronted, Mrs. Bayor stared suspiciously at Ally a moment. "Theodore isn't my husband," she stated firmly, spacing the words out as if suspecting Ally might be slow. "Theodore is my *son*."

Hearing it confirmed again made Ally feel a little sick, and she placed her hand against her stomach, trying to ease her sudden nausea. To think, if she'd known the truth, that night with Troy might never have happened….

"Why on earth would you think he's my husband?" Mrs. Bayor demanded, interrupting her thoughts.

Because a low-down liar told me so, Ally thought grimly. Aloud she said, "I'm sorry. It was just a—natural mistake."

Mrs. Bayor looked slightly mollified, so Ally added, "And we weren't stalking Theodore. I had a business proposition I wanted to put to him."

"Oh." That appeared to appease the older woman even more. "Well, I'm in charge of the store, so any business should be discussed with me. What is it that you propose?"

I'd like your son to pretend to be married to me for a few months, or possibly longer, so I can get full control over some land I inherited. Even in her head, the words sounded insane. Ally sighed. "Never mind. It was a stupid idea."

Mrs. Bayor's brow lowered again and she looked as if she might persist, but just then Lisa the reluctant salesclerk returned.

"Pregnancy tests are a *personal* item," Lisa declared, punctuating her announcement with a decisive snap of her gum as she dumped the boxes back on the counter. "Like baby powder, or sunscreen, or—" her gaze flickered over Mrs. Bayor's face "—or hair-waxing kits. And, although customer satisfaction is our goal," Lisa assured Ally woodenly, "we do *not* give refunds for personal items at this store." She blew a huge purple bubble, popped it and pulled the sticky residue off her lips. She held the gum in her purple-tipped fingers as she asked, "So d'ya wanna buy these, or not?"

Ally bought three.

At least, she consoled herself as she left the store, Mrs. Bayor didn't know too many people in Tangleweed yet. So she probably wouldn't mention the encounter to any—

Oh, good lord! Was that Sue Ellen?

Ally instinctively ducked around the corner of the building. Flattening against the hot stucco, she snuck a peek, returned to hiding.

Sue Ellen was sitting in a sedan parked right in front of the store.

Ally drew a deep breath, then crouching low, moving fast, keeping every car possible between herself and Sue Ellen, she snuck to her truck. She unlocked the door, then slid in and immediately turned on the ignition. Hunched behind the wheel, she started off.

Sue Ellen didn't even glance her way…but as Ally drove past the front of the store, Ally saw Mrs. Bayor standing by the sedan, staring at her.

Ally's stomach clenched. Not good, but not completely hopeless, Ally decided, mentally reviewing her conversation with the woman. She'd never given Mrs. Bayor her name, so what could she say?

Ally drove fast during the long trip home, hoping to get back to the ranch before her brothers missed her. But when she reached Tangleweed, she turned in at the Piggly Wiggly as automatically as a horse heading toward a bucket of oats. No matter what else was happening in her life, she still had four men to feed.

Less than twenty minutes later—by not making eye contact with anyone in the store—Ally had finished her speed shopping. She was putting her grocery bags in the bed of the pickup when she heard the throbbing growl of a well-tuned diesel. Goose bumps prickled on Ally's arms. She glanced over her shoulder and—*please, no*—saw Troy O'Malley's gleaming black truck coasting through the parking lot.

Despite the sun beating down hot enough to melt the asphalt beneath her thin-soled sandals, dismay shivered along her spine. Ally hurriedly turned back to her cart, pretending to be intent on stuffing her bags in the truck. *Oh, please, oh, please, oh, please! Let him just drive past!* The big truck glided behind her. She held her breath…but her prayer went unanswered. The truck's motor shifted to a rumbling purr as it drew to a stop.

"Hey, there, blondie."

Ally almost reached up to her brunette hair before she remembered. Oh, yeah. Misty's wig. She drew a deep breath, then—struggling to keep her expression blank—turned to face Troy.

He was wearing a black hat—perfectly suited to his true character—and sunglasses; the mirrored kind that reflected tiny twin images of herself standing by her tailgate with her face half hidden by her own sunglasses. She pushed them higher on her nose, thankful he couldn't see her eyes. She couldn't see his, either, but she felt the heat of his gaze as it ran over her, from the tips of her toes, up over her jeans, to her blue tank top to—

Was he staring at her breasts? Remembering them *naked?*

Flushing at the thought, she casually scooped the last brown paper bag from the cart, cradling it in front of her as she replied in as cool a voice as she could manage, "Hey, Troy."

He had the sleeves of his blue chambray shirt rolled up. One tanned muscular arm was draped across the steering wheel, the other rested on the rolled-down window as he leaned toward her. He slipped off his glasses and she almost flinched as his piercing green gaze met hers directly. "So, how've you been?"

"Just fine." Determined to appear as nonchalant as he did, Ally set the bag in the truck, then lifted the tailgate, locking it into place. Turning, she leaned against it, crossing her arms over her breasts. "You?"

"Not so good," he admitted. "You probably heard what happened at the rodeo."

"What?" she asked—just as if she hadn't subtly pried every detail of the rodeo and the fall Troy had taken out of Kyle, and didn't already know the answer.

"I really jacked up my knee."

And did you hurt your fingers, too? Is that why you never called? Or were you too busy laughing over what a fool I'd been? "Bull riding?" she inquired politely.

"Yeah. During the very first go-round, wouldn't you know." His voice dropped lower and picked up a husky note. "The morning after that night we spent together."

Her stomach dipped. She didn't say anything, and Troy's green eyes glinted at her intently from beneath his black hat brim.

"I just escaped my doctor—he's held me hostage in Dallas the past three weeks, torturing me—"

Yippee for the doctor!

"—with electric stimulus, water therapy—" he grinned wryly "—you name it, and he tried it."

Thumbscrews? The rack?

"But his efforts must have helped," Troy continued, "'cause he's got me walking again, and the knee feels better every day."

"Good for you," Ally said, trying not to sound sarcastic.

She must have succeeded because his eyes darkened and grew heavy-lidded, as his gaze moved over her again. "Yeah, well, I headed home just as soon as he released me this morning and— Look—" his voice assumed the intimate tone that made her stomach drop and then do somersaults "—do you have time for a bite to eat? We really need to talk."

Ally considered his request in silence, fighting to appear impassive as she studied the stern set of his mouth, the determined line of his jaw. In her opinion, the time for talking had long passed. But Troy didn't look like he'd take no for an answer.

Sure enough, when she didn't agree right away, his wide mouth tightened. "We need to talk, Ally," he repeated, his tone hardening a bit. "Get a few things sorted out."

No, Ally decided, he wasn't going to give up easily. So she shrugged and straightened. "Sure. Why don't you meet me at Daisy's?"

"Okay." His mouth relaxed into a faint smile that made the corners of his green eyes crinkle invitingly. "Want to ride over with me?"

She shook head and made a shooing gesture with her hand. "No, you go on over and get us a table. I need to pick up one more thing at the hardware, and then I'll join you. If you don't mind waiting?"

"Don't mind at all. See you in a bit." He touched the brim of his hat to her, put his truck in gear—then paused. "Oh, and Ally…"

"Yes?" she asked, forcing a smile.

"I like your hair."

Her smile almost slipped, but she managed to maintain it, waving as he drove away.

He turned the corner onto Main Street, and her smile disappeared. She climbed into her truck and started the ignition. Jerking into First, she peeled out of the parking lot, heading in the opposite direction, driving out of town as quickly as she dared.

No way did she want to share a meal with him. Like that old saying warned, if you sup with the devil you'd better have a long-handled spoon. And even in Texas, there wasn't a spoon long enough to handle Troy Michael O'Malley.

Scrub brush and stunted trees flashed past the window as, pedal-to-the-metal, Ally raced for home. Even now, alone in the truck, heat burned in her cheeks as she thought back to that fiasco of a night. How could she have been so—so stupid? Gone to his motel room, kissed him—gotten naked! She'd been disappointed and embarrassed that he'd fallen asleep on her; hurt and upset that he hadn't bothered to call. For the past three weeks she'd thought about that night at least forty—no, make that fifty—times a day with so many emotions churning through her when she did, she'd become confused about exactly how she felt.

But not any longer. After learning the truth about Theodore Bayor and his mother, rage burned away any lingering uncertainty. She never ever wanted to see the low-down, lying dog Troy O'Malley again!

Barely slowing, she skidded through the Circle C gates and, a few minutes later, braked in front of the ranch house in a small flurry of dust and gravel. She jumped out of the cab, grabbed a couple of bags from the truck bed, and carried them past Cole's black lab, Buster, who was lying on the porch.

Seeing Buster, she figured Cole was home, and when she reached the kitchen doorway, she saw Kyle was, too. They'd apparently been home awhile, because their hats were off, tossed on the kitchen table. Cole was leaning against the counter, big arms crossed, watching Kyle, who was talking on his cell phone. Both blue gazes whipped around, fastening on her as she walked in.

Cole straightened, and with an abrupt goodbye, Kyle snapped his phone shut and stepped toward her.

"Where on earth have you been?" Cole demanded.

"Out," Ally replied succinctly. She set the bags on the counter and headed outside for more—with her brothers hot on her heels.

"We were worried about you," Kyle said, taking away the bags she picked up, while Cole gathered the rest from the truck bed. Ally slammed the tailgate closed and headed back into the house, her brothers still trailing her.

Cole was still frowning, and Kyle still talking. "There're some strange rumors goin' round," he told her. "I just hung up with Jerry Cook at the feed store and he says Willie Pitts told him that Sue Ellen ran into you at the pharmacy in Austin and you told her you're pregnant!"

Sue Ellen must have phoned her news in, Ally reflected sourly. Proving once again that gossip in Tangleweed traveled faster than a blue-bellied lizard skittering up a wall.

"That's ridiculous," she said shortly. "I never told Sue Ellen any such thing."

She stalked into the kitchen. She headed toward the table and started pulling groceries from the bags—hoping against hope that would end the matter.

It didn't. "How did a rumor like that get started?" Cole wondered, his dark brows low over his eyes as he set his bags next to the ones Kyle had retrieved.

Kyle shook his head and cracked his knuckles, beginning to pace. "I don't know—but I'd sure like to find out."

"Forget it," Ally advised them, gathering up cans of vegetables to put away. "It's not worth worrying about."

They didn't listen to her, of course. When did they ever listen? Ally wondered. She kept stacking cans of corn and beans in the cupboard, Cole and Kyle kept speculating and muttering angrily, until the twins came in.

Ally frowned at them, her heart dropping. "Shouldn't you all be out moving cattle?" she asked, trying to nudge them on their way.

"Luke got a call from Sarah," Linc told her, his voice clipped, his eyes meeting hers grimly. "About you."

Ally waited fatalistically to hear what Luke's current girl-friend had to say.

"She told me that Tammy Pitts said you have a bun in the oven," Luke elaborated before his twin could.

Ally lifted her chin but avoided their eyes. "Tammy Pitts is full of pure, unadulterated spite," she said, refusing to mince matters. "She's always saying something mean about someone."

No one argued with her summation of Tammy's character, but Linc said grimly, "I don't understand why she's going after you, but it pisses me off."

It pissed them all off. Her brothers stood in a loose circle surrounding the kitchen table discussing the matter as she diligently continued to empty the bags of groceries. The twins still had their hats on, and although Linc's was tilted down, partly concealing his expression, Luke's was pushed back, clearly revealing the angry bewilderment on his face. Kyle couldn't keep still. He kept pacing and cracking his knuckles, while Cole had settled into a lethal stillness that alarmed Ally more than the rest of her brothers' reactions combined.

"Jerry said you supposedly hooked up with some guy that you met at Big Bob's," Kyle told Ally, and gave a short laugh. "I told him you've never even been in that hellhole and to shut his damn mouth."

From the corner of her eye, Ally saw Cole give a start at the mention of Big Bob's. She began digging in another brown bag, trying to avoid his penetrating stare. It didn't work.

"I know you went out with Misty that night I found her at Big Bob's, Al," Cole said slowly, "and that you drove my truck home, since it was here when she dropped me off. But where did you go off to? And who did you take off with?"

Her other brothers stiffened at this information, turning almost in unison to stare at her, waiting for her reply.

Suddenly, Ally was completely fed up. Swinging around, she abandoned the groceries to confront Cole face on. "Where did *you* go?" she demanded. "When I came out of the restroom at Big Bob's, Misty was gone—and so were you. So where did you two go? Did you even come home that night?"

Going on the offense worked…for about two seconds. Cole blinked at her in surprise, then his dark brows lowered again and his jaw tightened. His hands fisted on his hips. "We aren't talking about me. I'm thirty years old and well able to take care of myself. While you—"

"While I'm twenty-four and just as able to take care of *myself!*" Ally answered, putting her hands on her hips, too. She hated—*hated!*—the way they were all looking at her, with varying degrees of concern, anger and disbelief stamped on their rugged features. She hated even more the rising edge of hysteria she could hear in her own voice. She was losing it here. *Not* the best way to demonstrate she was a rational human being, totally in control of herself and the situation.

Taking a deep breath, she strove to stay calm. "I'm an adult, too—just as much as the rest of you." Her voice as firm as she could make it, she added, "What I do—and whomever I do it with—is none of your business."

For a long moment, no one spoke. Then Cole sighed, dropping his hands to his sides. "Sorry, Al. You're right. We all just got carried away."

Ally could feel her eyes mist as the others mumbled apologies, as well. She cleared her throat to say huskily, "That's okay. I understand. And in any case—" she turned back to the groceries, picking up a bag to indicate the discussion was *over* "—there's nothing to worry about here. Everything is *fine*."

Tension made her movements jerky. The bag tilted and three small boxes—blue, beige and pink—tumbled to the floor.

The pink one landed faceup, displaying a young woman smiling at the small stick she held. The words Pregnancy Test were printed clearly at the top.

Luke choked. Cole growled. Linc muttered a curse. Kyle, who'd automatically bent to pick the boxes up, recoiled, jerking back his hand.

Ally stifled a groan. If the boxes had been a pile of rattlers chock-full of venom and ready to strike, the expressions of stunned horror on her brothers' faces couldn't have been greater. They were still staring at the boxes, standing frozen in a bug-eyed tableau when a sound intruded—a loud, angry pounding on the front door, followed by a man's voice raised in harsh demand.

"Ally? Ally Cabrerra! I know you're in there, Ally, so you'd better come open this door before I break it down. I heard some news in Daisy's and— Damn it! *Open this door!* We need to talk *big time* about that night in the motel!"

Cole lifted his head like a wolf scenting prey. He glanced from the boxes to the door, then nodded curtly at his brothers, his eyes narrowing to gleaming blue slits.

"Go get him," he ordered.

Chapter Six

"When buying a bull, consider long and hard before making your final selection. Do not be influenced by aggrandized advertising. Sperm count and staying power are more important than fulsome rhetoric, and reputation doesn't always equal results...."

—*Successful Breeding: A Guide for the Cattleman*

Her brothers had embarrassed her before. But nothing compared to the humiliation Ally felt when Kyle and Luke re-entered the kitchen escorting Troy O'Malley limping on crutches between them, with Linc guarding the rear.

Cole stepped forward to meet them. He grabbed at Troy's shirt—and Troy grabbed back, dropping a crutch. Cussing and shouting, the others leaped to separate the scuffling men, and somehow Ally ended up at Troy's side, facing her brothers.

"Knock it off!" she said fiercely, shoving at one rock-hard shoulder, then another, glaring at the group. "All of you!"

Troy's green eyes were snapping, his eyebrows slanted in a fierce frown. Cole was so angry that Ally could see his chest rise as he drew in a shuddering breath. But when Linc said quietly, "He's on crutches, bro," Cole released his hold on Troy. Troy reluctantly returned the favor, and Cole stepped back.

"You've got a lot to explain, O'Malley," Cole stated, his expression harder than Ally had ever seen it. He reached down, grabbed up one of the boxes. "And you can start with this!"

He threw the box at Troy, who automatically caught it with one hand. Troy juggled it against his chest, wobbling a bit on his remaining crutch. "What the—" He glanced down, bit off a curse. "So the gossip at the diner was true." Lifting his head, he ignored everyone else to look straight at Ally. "You should have called me."

His voice was deadly quiet. His tanned fingers white where he clutched the pink box.

"Why?" Ally asked, lifting her chin in challenge. "The phone works two ways, you know. And I sure didn't hear mine ringing off the hook."

"Then you weren't listening very hard."

She choked. "Oh! You're such a liar—"

"No, he's not," Cole cut in unexpectedly. "Not about this, anyway. I cleared his messages. I didn't know about—" he indicated the boxes in an abrupt gesture "—any of this. I thought he was calling to bug you about Bride's Price."

Ally stared at her oldest brother in amazement, not knowing what to say, where to even begin to list how arrogant, how controlling Cole had been. Before she could try, Troy said harshly, "That's no excuse."

Ally nodded, putting her hands on her hips. She totally agreed.

Once again Cole had been *way* out of line. Ally glanced at Troy to tell him his remark was dead-on, only to discover he hadn't been talking about Cole. Oh, no, not at all. Troy's hard stare—his accusing words—were directed at *her.*

She sputtered in surprise. "No excuse? But Cole didn't tell me you'd called—"

"That doesn't matter." Anger burned in the green eyes that met hers straight on, and Troy's lips had thinned to a flat, hard line. When he spoke, the words emerged through his set white teeth. "It wasn't right of your brother not to tell you I called, but in any event—"

Ally gasped when he dared—*dared!*—to point a reproving finger at her.

"—*you* should have called me when you suspected you were pregnant. No ifs, ands or buts about it."

Ally opened her mouth, closed it and glanced around, wondering which of her brothers would take him apart first. To her astonishment and growing fury, all her bullheaded brothers were nodding in agreement, disapproval plainly stamped on all their faces as they stared at her. Even Cole—the biggest control freak Texas had ever produced—obviously agreed with his enemy on this particular subject one hundred percent.

Unbelievable.

Ally clenched her fists, then forced herself to take a deep breath and relax her fingers, trying to calm down once again.

"Look," she said, glancing from one stern masculine face to another, "this whole conversation is just—just ridiculous. Nothing happened in that motel that night."

Silence. Until Troy drawled softly, "And you call me a liar."

Ally flushed. "I—it—all right, then! Nothing happened that would get me pregnant," she amended.

Even this embarrassing admission made no difference. Not one disbelieving expression changed.

Ally gritted her teeth. Deciding to ignore her idiot brothers for the moment, she fastened her gaze on Troy's hard face, meeting his narrowed green gaze without flinching. "Okay, let me make this clear: *You are not going to be a father.* At least not by me."

If anything, Troy's expression grew grimmer. He disregarded the last part of her statement to demand, "Are you saying you've been with another man since that night?"

Ally choked, her flush flaring hotter in her cheeks. "No! Of course not!" Seeing his eyes glint, she realized that hadn't come out quite right and added hastily, "I mean I'm not pregnant at all. There's not the slightest possibility that I could be."

His eyes didn't waver from hers. "That's not how I remember it."

"Then your memory is obviously faulty."

"A little," he acknowledged unexpectedly. Crossing his arms, he studied her face shrewdly. "But if what you say is true—that you couldn't possibly be pregnant—"

"It is!"

"If that's true," he repeated, ignoring her interjection, "then why did you buy three pregnancy kits?"

Ally stared at him, her eyes widening. It was a simple question—one that would settle this matter immediately.

And she couldn't answer.

"Because I—you—I just—" She glanced almost frantically past one waiting male face to another. "You all are just—oh, get out of my way!" Stiff-arming the twins from her path, she raced toward the nearest sanctuary.

A few seconds later, the bathroom door slammed.

In the kitchen, a long silence ensued. The men glanced at one another. Then Luke finally said with a sigh what they all were thinking, "She's pregnant, all right."

Cole straightened abruptly. "I'll go talk to her." He headed to the door, but Troy swung his crutch across the doorjamb, barring the way.

"I'll talk to her," Troy stated. "You've interfered enough, Cabrerra." And without waiting to see how any of the brothers reacted, he lowered his crutch to follow Ally, the pregnancy test still clamped in his hand as he limped down the hall.

In the bathroom, Ally shot the small bolt lock home, then marched over to the old claw-footed tub and climbed in. Fully clothed, she leaned back and shut her eyes, trying to concentrate solely on the feel of the cool porcelain against her heated body. To forget about the pack of mule-headed males in her kitchen.

A sharp rap sounded on the bathroom door.

"Ally, it's me. Troy." A pause and then another sharp rap. "Open up. We still need to talk."

Ally's eyes opened a slit. Did he have to keep saying that? And keep following her around? Her fingers clenched around the smooth, curved sides of the tub. "Go away!" she ordered.

"Not gonna happen," he drawled. Even through the barrier of the wooden door panels, Ally could hear the thread of steel buried in his laconic tone. "We still have things to discuss."

"I have nothing to say to you."

"That's fine, because I have plenty to say to you."

Ally didn't want to hear it. She sat upright and defiantly grabbed two rolls of toilet paper off the open shelf next to the tub. She pressed them to her ears. Damn, she should have bought two-ply. The rolls barely muffled Troy's voice as he told her, "I'll be happy to have this conversation shouted through the door for everyone to hear…or you can open up and give us some privacy."

Resentfully, Ally climbed out of the tub and threw the bolt.

Hearing the small click, Troy immediately pushed the door

open, crowding her back. Without waiting for an invitation, he came in and relocked the door.

For a bathroom, this one was fairly large, but Ally retreated as far from him as she could, bumping into the tub with the back of her knees.

Troy gave her as much space as possible, leaning his shoulders against the door as he studied her intently. Her honey-gold skin was still flushed with a rosy glow of embarrassment. Her dark, silky hair was tousled. Her blue eyes were stormy. Unconsciously, his gaze drifted past her delicate collarbones and the sweet curves of her breasts to her abdomen.

His heart kicked up a beat. Her waist still looked slim and her hipbones jutted against the thin cloth above her low-slung jeans. Her belly—

She crossed her arms suddenly, hiding it from view, and Troy's gaze jerked up to meet hers.

"You can stop staring," she said in a level tone. "I'm not pregnant."

"How do you know?"

"I just do."

Troy slowly set the pink box he was holding on the sink. She anticipated what he was going to say, and got in first. "I'm not taking that test."

He considered her a moment. Her voice was calm, but her shoulders were tense, her arms still crossed to hide her middle. Her expression was filled with stubborn determination.

"Look," he said, keeping his own tone reasonable, "we've both made mistakes here."

"You certainly have," she shot back. "Beginning with lying to me about Theodore Bayor being married."

"I didn't lie—I didn't," he insisted when she made a scoffing sound. "I just let you assume—what you chose to assume."

"You tricked me."

"Okay, maybe a little," he allowed, "but it was for your own good."

He probably should have phrased that better, Troy thought, when she gasped in indignation, but his patience was wearing thin. "C'mon, Ally," he said in exasperation, "you have to admit that marrying me made a lot more sense than involving a stranger like Bayor. After all, I'm the one who wants that lease. And now that you might be pregnant…"

"I told you it's not possible."

He gave a short laugh. "Anything's possible when two people make love without using birth control." Never again, he vowed, looking at her white face. Never again would he be so stupid about drinking, using painkillers. He ran his hand through his hair and drew a deep breath. "I admit, a lot of what happened in that motel room is kind of a blur. I'd had too much to drink, and I'd taken painkillers on top of that, but— Damn it! I *always* use a condom." He eyed her in frustration, silently cursing himself. "But I didn't that night—did I?"

He thought she wouldn't answer, but after a long pause she finally admitted, "No, you didn't."

"And you're not on anything, are you?"

"No," she said reluctantly.

"So let's face it—" he held up his hand to stop her as she tried to interrupt "—whether we like it or not, the possibility exists." A very good possibility, in his opinion, considering not only had she gone out and bought three pregnancy tests, she was more emotional than he'd ever seen her—just like a pregnant woman.

Again, his heart bucked at the thought, but he kept his face impassive, his tone reasonable, as he continued, "Which gives us just one more good reason to go ahead with your plan."

"My plan?" she repeated blankly.

"Yeah, your plan to marry me. To get control of your inheritance."

She sat down on the edge of the tub, her arms still crossed over her stomach. "You're kidding, right?"

"No, I'm not kidding," he said, his tone sharpening despite himself. "I'm dead serious here. I think we should do it."

"For the last time," she said through gritted teeth, "I'm not pregnant."

"Okay, but even if you aren't, you haven't changed your mind, have you? You still want to give me that lease, don't you?"

"Yes, but—"

"And Cole hasn't given in, has he? Given you control of Bride's Price?"

"No, but—are you sure this is just about the lease?" she asked suspiciously. "And not about…anything else?"

"I didn't even know about all this—" he tapped the pink box "—when I asked you to meet me at Daisy's to discuss the lease and your plan to marry." *And to talk to you about the night at the motel.* "I would have spoken to you sooner—" *to apologize for passing out so quickly* "—if Cole hadn't interfered. But when I couldn't get you on the phone, I decided to wait until I could drive, and come see you in person." *To try to persuade you to go to bed with me again, as soon as possible.*

She studied his face, letting the silence spin out—and Troy realized he was clenching his jaw. He forced himself to relax. Casually, he crossed his arms, tucking his hands under his armpits to resist the almost overwhelming urge to grab her and kiss her and *make* her agree to marry him.

He waited. And waited. And—when he simply couldn't stand her silence one second longer—he asked again, "So what do you say, Ally? Do you still want Bride's Price?"

"Oh, yes," she admitted slowly. "I still want Bride's Price."

"That's great." He smiled at her—the most disarming, persuasive, innocent smile he could muster. "So, will you marry me? Do we have a deal?"

Ally met his eyes. She studied them a second before her gaze dropped to his mouth.

Her blue eyes narrowed. "All right," she said softly. "We have a deal."

Chapter Seven

"Remember: Mounting is not a guarantee that penetration has occurred."
—*Successful Breeding: A Guide for the Cattleman*

Once he'd secured Ally's agreement, Troy took action. He hustled Ally to the Meyer county courthouse in less than three days.

Ally's brothers accompanied her to town to witness the brief civil service, and Troy's grandfather was there, as well. Standing between the twins in the courthouse foyer waiting to go before the judge, Ally smoothed her hand nervously over the white dress Misty had sent to the Circle C the day before with Stan Gunderland, the longtime Sanderson foreman, in response to Ally's phone message inviting Misty to the hastily arranged wedding ceremony.

Ally appreciated the loan of the dress; it helped her confidence. Short and strapless, with a fitted bodice and a full skirt that fell softly to her knees, it was perfect for the occasion and the hot sunny afternoon. But her confidence would have been boosted even higher if Misty had been present to offer some feminine support.

Misty, however, had called early that morning to tell Ally she couldn't attend. Startled awake before dawn by the chirp of the cell phone Cole had given her, Ally had grabbed it off her night table, blearily thinking Troy was calling to cancel. She hadn't known if she was relieved or disappointed to hear Misty's voice on the line.

"I'm sorry, but I'm going to have to miss the wedding, Ally," Misty said without preamble. "I just can't leave Daddy. He's still not doing well."

Ally sat up in bed, tugging the sheet over her up-drawn knees to ward off the cool morning air, and pushing her tangled hair off her face. "I'm so sorry, Mist. Is there anything I can do? Anyone I should call?"

"Thanks for offering, but no," Misty assured her, adding in a grateful tone, "You've done enough already, buying those pregnancy kits. I don't even want to imagine Daddy having to worry about me right now when he needs to be concentrating on getting better. But oh, Ally! I never thought everyone would think *you* were pregnant." Misty's voice turned fretful. "And now you're marrying Troy because of it—"

"That's not why I'm marrying him," Ally interrupted her. "I'm doing it to get control of my inheritance, like we discussed."

"So Troy knows you're not pregnant?"

"I told him I wasn't, "Ally answered truthfully. It wasn't her fault if he'd been too cocksure—now there was a word that fit!—to believe her.

There was a short silence, then Misty asked softly, "Does Cole—do the rest of your brothers—know that you bought the tests for me?"

"Nope. It's none of their business," Ally said firmly—and she was determined to keep it that way. At least for now. She added, "But, Misty, Cole will need to know eventually if—"

"I know, I know." Misty sounded miserable. "And I'll tell him, I promise. But I just can't deal with him right now on top of—everything else."

"So…" Ally tried to resist, but couldn't help asking, "did you take any of the tests?"

Silence loomed on the other end of the line. Then, "No, not yet," Misty answered, her tone half defensive, half guilty. "I planned to take one as soon as Stan brought them back after delivering your dress, but I haven't even opened the gift box you disguised them in yet. I—well, I guess I want to put off knowing for sure, at least for a little while."

She'd hung up with a quick goodbye before Ally could argue with her decision—not that Ally would have. She didn't blame Misty at all for wanting to delay bad news. Ally wished she'd delayed a few things herself. Particularly this wedding.

She glanced around nervously and accidentally met Cole's gaze. When he looked away without smiling, she immediately did the same, swallowing past the lump in her throat. Ever since discovering the pregnancy tests, the Cabrerra males had conveyed their disapproval of her perceived misbehavior by maintaining a distant politeness. Although their attitude made her angry—who were they to judge her actions?—it also hurt.

Yet, it also reassured her she was doing the right thing. It had become clear during that uproar over the pregnancy tests that her brothers, especially Cole, were more controlling than she'd ever realized. Marriage was the easiest, the best solution to her problem: her ticket to escape their constant interference, so she could finally live her own life.

Determined to ignore her brother, she focused on Troy,

standing about twenty yards away with his grandfather. Both men wore suits—Troy the charcoal-gray he'd worn to Aunt Eileen's funeral, and Mick, a Western-style tan one. Mick had his head tilted forward as he talked to his grandson, his grim gaze fixed on Troy's face as they stood near one of the large windows that graced the old building. Both men held their Stetsons, and the sunlight streaming through the wavy glass made Mick's thick gray hair gleam like a metal helmet, and burnished Troy's hair to a glossy brown.

Troy didn't have his crutches, but his slight limp led Ally to assume he still wore some sort of brace on his knee. He was frowning at the ground—Ally wondered if his knee was hurting— when he suddenly looked up, his gaze intercepting hers.

She quickly glanced away.

Across the room, Troy's frown deepened at her action and he shifted restlessly, barely listening as his grandfather rambled on by his side.

"I'm proud of you, son. It takes a real man to take action, to do whatever needs to be done to get what they want…."

Troy nodded absently, his attention fixed on the dark-haired, slim figure standing at the other end of the room. The jolt of hungry desire he'd felt on first seeing her raced through him again. Hot damn, she looked beautiful. She had on a white dress—not a long, frilly dress that he'd vaguely imagined all brides wore—but a short, simple sundress that left her slender golden arms and straight shoulders bare and made her long, sexy legs look even longer.

"For sixty years I've been trying to get that land back…."

A small gold cross encircled her slim neck, and she'd left her hair loose, hanging around her shoulders. She had her slender hands clasped in front of her and was twisting them together. Not wringing them, exactly, but— Flowers! Damn it, he'd forgotten flowers!

"Those hills up past the Veil Falls are thick with game. Javelina, spike buck, turkey…"

Every bride needed flowers to hold. How could he have forgotten something like that? Well, he consoled himself, he'd buy her a big bunch when they reached Kauai. Wouldn't she be surprised to find out where he was taking her for a honeymoon? Maybe she'd give him a big smile then…'cause she sure wasn't giving him one now.

"In the fall, I figure we'll invite Senator Adams and his aide for a hunting party. Those Washington politicians sure enjoy hunting…."

Hoping she'd at least look at him again, Troy continued to watch her, but her gaze remained fixed on the open doors of the courthouse. Probably thinking about bolting through them, he thought grimly. Yeah, she was looking pretty scared—and her brothers more tight-lipped with every second that passed. Troy shifted, mentally debating whether to check with the bailiff to see if the justice of the peace was ready for them yet. He wanted this wedding ceremony over and done with as quickly as possible before Ally changed her mind.

"…Getting that Cabrerra gal knocked up, pushing her into a wedding to get a claim on the land—" Jerked out of his preoccupation, Troy's head snapped up, as his grandfather slapped him on the shoulder. "That takes balls, son." Chuckling at his own play on words, Mick slapped Troy again. "Real balls."

"I'm not marrying her for the land," Troy told him bluntly, realizing as he said it the truth of the statement. Not once since learning he was going to be a father had he given a thought to Bride's Price. Staking his claim to the baby—not the land—had been the goal driving him.

"Sure you aren't, son." Mick winked at him, but his voice turned grim as he added, "Just be careful you don't get tangled in your own snare. Get in, and then get out of this marriage, as quickly as possible."

Before Troy could correct him again, the door to the judges' chambers opened and the bailiff poked his bald head out to nod at Troy. Troy returned the gesture with a sigh of relief. Finally, they could get this settled.

Excusing himself, he immediately started across the room to where Ally was standing. Ignoring the way the Cabrerra brothers glared and closed ranks around her as he approached, Troy limped straight up to her and held out his hand. "It's time."

For a moment—a long moment—she stared at his hand without moving. But just when he was about to reach for her, she put her hand in his. A surprising surge of satisfaction filled Troy as his fingers closed around hers. Holding her small hand firmly, he led her from her brothers toward the big doors shielding the courtroom.

By no means was the civil ceremony that followed romantic. The judge looked bored, the little gray-haired woman recording the proceedings appeared harried, and Ally's brothers and his grandfather remained grim. Troy felt determined, while Ally still had the anxious, hunted expression she'd been wearing since she arrived.

She looked pale, and her slender hand felt cold in his grasp. Troy tightened his grip on her fingers as the judge inquired, "Do you have a ring?"

Troy saw Ally shake her head—at the same time as he nodded. She glanced at him in surprise as he pulled a ring from his pocket.

Seeing the circlet of diamonds, her blue eyes widened. Her hand jerked convulsively in his, but Troy held on tight. Giving her fingers a warning squeeze, he slipped the ring on, his heart pounding as he said his vows. It pounded even harder when her turn came, and she hesitated, biting her lip as she glanced at the small group surrounding them.

Troy drew a deep breath and set his jaw. She was going to back out; he could feel it. He squeezed her hand again, silently demanding she go through with it. Her eyes lifted to his…and stayed there as she started speaking. Her fingers trembled in his grasp, and her voice was low but steady as she repeated the words that bound them together.

"I, Allyson Eileen Cabrerra, take thee Troy Michael O'Malley, to be my lawfully wedded husband…"

It wasn't until the judge said the words that sealed the deal "—I now pronounce you husband and wife—" that Troy finally released the breath he'd been holding, and turned to take Ally in his arms. The judge hadn't instructed them to do so, but it suddenly seemed important to kiss her. To publicly demonstrate to everyone that Ally—and the baby she carried—were now his.

He settled his mouth firmly on hers. He didn't intend to make a big production of it…but she felt so damn good pressed up against him; her lips were so soft, she tasted so sweet, he forgot his noble intentions. He kissed her deeply, thoroughly—until a forceful cough from one of her brothers reminded him of their audience.

Reluctantly, he broke the kiss and raised his head. Her long, dark lashes lifted, revealing languorous blue eyes. Slowly, she smiled at him—a real smile—and the gray-haired court clerk sighed loudly in wistful appreciation.

Ally blinked at the small sound—then tensed in Troy's arms. Heat flooding her cheeks, she hurriedly dropped her gaze from Troy's and removed her arms from around his neck. She couldn't believe they'd kissed like that—right in front of everyone. She straightened so she was no longer leaning on Troy and, even though her legs felt shaky, forced herself to stand alone.

She accepted the judge's good wishes and an impulsive hug from the now starry-eyed little court clerk in a daze.

Once again, Troy's kiss seemed to have scrambled something

in her brain. It wasn't until their small party was in the foyer and Mick had left, that Ally's thoughts began to clear.

Linc's voice broke through the haze, and she realized that he'd been talking to her for a few moments already.

"…So you can use the wagon, Al," Linc said in his low drawl. "Take it for as long as you want. You'll need something to get around in."

The unexpected offer made Ally's throat tighten. They only had three vehicles running at the Circle C at present—the battered blue truck, an old Jeep the twins kept going with baling wire and curses, and Linc's vintage station wagon. As a teenager, he'd found the old Ford Falcon dumped in a ditch and had been meticulously restoring it ever since with whatever time and money he could spare.

Ally knew Linc loved that car. Lending it to her was a big sacrifice on his part. Smiling tremulously, she touched his arm gently. "Thanks, Linc. I appreciate it."

His habitually cynical expression softened as he covered her hand, giving it a pat.

Then Ally felt Troy's arm slide around her waist. "I appreciate the offer, too," he said rather curtly, cinching her closer to his side and away from her brother. "But Ally can use my truck. I'll have my Lexus brought from Dallas if we find we need another vehicle."

The softness disappeared from Linc's face. His dark blue eyes narrowed, and his mouth twisted in his crooked smile. "Fine." He glanced at his sister. "But if you change your mind, Al, the offer stands."

Ally nodded, managing to choke out, "Thanks again, Linc."

Troy hesitated, then looked at her brothers again. He said in a more cordial tone, "Ally and I would like to invite you all to an early dinner at the steak house in Fredericksburg for a brief celebration."

Although this was the first Ally had heard of the plan, her heart lifted, only to drop again in disappointment as Cole shook his head.

"Thanks, but we can't." It was Cole's turn to be curt. "We have to get home. Al. Troy."

He nodded, then turned and headed to the door, the rest of his brothers on his heels. Without thinking, Ally started to follow, only to be brought up short by a tug on her dress.

She looked inquiringly over her shoulder. Troy returned the look in exasperation. "Where do you think you're going?"

"To the Circle C."

The exasperation on his face was echoed in his voice as he said, "We're married now, Ally. Remember that ceremony we went through less than fifteen minutes ago? When I gave you this?" He caught her left hand. Raising it in front of her face, he tapped the sparkling band on her ring finger. "Part of the purpose of that entire exercise was to establish that we're a couple now, so you can gain control of Bride's Price. Did you think you'd just go your way and I'd go mine?"

"No." *Yes*. Panic flickered through her as she saw her brothers disappear through the courthouse door. They were leaving her behind; they'd never done that before.

She needed to go with them, to finish packing. She tugged slightly, trying to pull free of Troy's grip. "I need to go back to the Circle C."

His voice was implacable. "No, you don't."

"Yes, I do. I need to get my stuff."

"Fine." Still holding her hand, he started limping toward the door. "I'll drive you."

He released her to slip his hat on as they stepped into the bright Texas sunlight. Ally glanced around, but her brothers were gone.

Troy grabbed her hand again and started across the wide

courthouse porch. "We'll stop at the Circle C to pick up your luggage and then head out to Dallas." He flashed her his wide, white grin. "From there, I thought we'd catch a flight out to honeymoon in Kauai—"

"What? No!" This time Ally dug in her heels, forcing him to stop or drag her down the broad stone steps of the courthouse.

He elected to stop. "No? You don't want to go to Kauai?"

"No!"

His grin faded. He looked disappointed for a moment, but immediately rallied. "Okay, what about Europe? Is your passport current?"

"No, my passport isn't current—I don't even have one! And I don't want to go to Europe, anyway."

The exasperated look crept back. "So where do you want to honeymoon?"

Ally stared, her eyes widening as she realized he was serious—that he wasn't just kidding around. He obviously expected them to go off on a honeymoon, just like a normal married couple!

They should have talked about this, she realized, slightly unnerved by the gleam in his eyes. But the marriage ceremony itself had consumed so much of her thoughts, she hadn't really considered much beyond it. Or rather, she had, but Troy hadn't been in her mental imaginings of the future at all.

So when he repeated, "Ally, I asked you where you want to go," she told him.

"I'm going to Bride's Price. You can go to…wherever you please."

Troy tried to talk her out of it. On the entire drive to the Circle C to pick up her stuff, he alternated between arguing, cajoling and demanding that she forget about Bride's Price.

Her brothers weren't at the ranch house when they pulled up. Ally suggested Troy wait in his truck, but he ignored her, still arguing as he trailed her into the house.

"You can't be serious," he stated, following her so closely up the stairs to her bedroom that he bumped her a couple of times. "What does Bride's Price have that Kauai doesn't?"

Ally stopped in her bedroom doorway to face him. "Privacy," she said. Then shut the door in his face and locked it.

She quickly changed into work clothes—cutoff shorts and a plain blue T-shirt—and gathered her hair into a ponytail. Then she picked up one of the boxes she'd started packing weeks ago after her argument with Cole, opened the door—and bumped into Troy. Again.

He was leaning against the jamb, his arms crossed over his wide chest, his hands tucked beneath his armpits, blocking her path. She'd thought changing out of her dress would put things back to normal, ease her unsettled feeling and douse the possessive spark in his green eyes. It didn't.

His gaze swept over her as he blocked her path, from the top of her ponytail down to her feet in her flat espadrilles, and the spark flared higher. "You look great," he said huskily.

Ally's stomach swooped. But before she could reply, Troy started nagging her again. "Instead of going to stay at Bride's Price, if you're really dead set against going away for our honeymoon, why don't we stay at my ranch house?" he asked coaxingly. "It'd be more fun."

"Your grandfather's ranch house, you mean," Ally retorted, shoving the box into his arms before turning around to grab another filled with clothes. Heading down the stairs with her growling, glowering shadow limping behind her, she added over her shoulder, "There's no way I'm ever going to stay with Old Mick. You can count on that."

"Fine, then we can go stay at my apartment in Dallas. It's a great place."

"Goody for you." She grabbed her hat off the peg by the door and slapped it on as they headed outside into the now waning sunshine. With Troy still dogging her heels, she strode across the porch and yard to drop her box in the bed of his truck, then turned to confront him. "Why would I want to go there—when I have a perfectly good home of my own?"

"What about supplies?" he demanded. "What about groceries—"

"Got them. I stocked up last time I went over."

That didn't stop him from arguing. Nothing stopped him. He kept trying to change her mind as they drove to the O'Malley spread so he could get his gear, too. They were nearly at the Running M when she finally managed to interrupt.

"Look, just because I'm going to Bride's Price doesn't mean you have to go, too. Cole will never know if you're there or not; so if you want to go to Dallas—"

She shrieked as Troy suddenly whipped the truck onto the shoulder of the highway. Dust flew, pebbles pinged against the hubcaps. Ally braced her hands against the dashboard, gasping in relief when the truck finally drew to a halt.

Troy rammed the gearshift into Park, but didn't bother turning off the motor as he swiveled to face her. Looking as grim as when he'd first seen the pregnancy tests in her kitchen, he pinned her with his green-eyed glare.

"Is that what you think of me?" he demanded, a muscle flexing in his square jaw. "That I'm the kind of low-life scum who'd leave a woman—my brand-new pregnant wife—all alone on an isolated ranch in a run-down farm house?"

"I have a phone," Ally protested a bit weakly.

Troy snorted. "Like that'll do a lot of good," he said scornfully, "with the reception you can expect in those hills. So just make up your mind to it, Ally, that until this baby comes, you're stuck with me. Where you go, I go."

And without giving her time to answer, he yanked into First, and pulled back out onto the highway.

Whew! Ally sat beside him, still a little stunned by the force of his sudden anger. She kept forgetting he thought she was pregnant. Maybe she should try again to set him straight…she slanted a glance at his angry face…or maybe not. Maybe when he'd cooled down a bit.

He was still running hot when they pulled in front of the O'Malley ranch house—which always reminded Ally of a miniature Tara wannabe that had wandered off its cotton plantation and somehow ended up in cattle country. With a curt "I'll be right back," Troy jumped out of the cab. By the time he returned, duffel bag in hand, she'd decided to wait until they'd reached Bride's Price and she was on her own turf before tackling the pregnancy topic one more time.

Troy took off again, and Ally settled in the soft leather seat with a sigh. It was only around five, but so much had happened that day, in such a short space of time, that tiredness settled over her like a cloak.

Next to her, Troy had subsided from demanding and cajoling, to occasional muttered growls interspersed by sullen silences. Well-versed in Manglish, Ally realized he'd entered deep sulking mode. Good. They needed to talk, but she wanted to recover a bit before starting another fight, so she stared silently out the window, hoping the endless vista of gently rolling hills would help soothe the unexpected sadness she was feeling.

She felt…almost homesick. Which was stupid; she was doing exactly what she wanted—breaking free of her brothers, becoming independent. But she couldn't help worrying about them a bit. Who would cook for them? Who'd clean up? She hadn't thought about that when she'd devised her plan.

A few minutes later, Troy glanced from the deserted highway to the woman at his side. How could she be so stubborn? He couldn't believe she'd pass up the chance to go to Kuaui—to Paris, to Rome, or even his luxurious condo in the heart of Dallas—to honeymoon in a small, shabby ranch house at the back of beyond. For days, as he rushed around getting their marriage license and her ring, arranging times and dates at the courthouse, he'd been looking forward to hours of extended lovemaking in a big comfortable bed.

But as the miles swept past, his disgruntled anger started to fade. He spared another glance at Ally. She looked so worn-out just sitting there, staring unseeingly out the window, obviously lost in thought. A few tendrils of her dark, silky hair curled against her soft cheek. The blue shirt she'd changed into had to be one of her brothers—it hung over her shoulders—but he'd swear the shorts she had on were the same cutoffs that had first caught his interest so long ago.

Her hands were in her lap, and she was absently twisting her wedding ring around on her finger as she stared out at the hills. The small sign of her nervousness softened his anger, and the sight of her bare, long golden legs stretched out lightened his mood even more as he thought about the night ahead. They were married now—he'd won the big battle. Did it really matter where they made love? After all, although some of his memories of the night in the motel were regrettably dim, enough remained to assure him they'd managed just fine on that narrow, single bed.

Hazy images of her soft breasts, her slender thighs, floated through his mind, and he decided to abandon the issue of how unreasonably stubborn she was being about going to Bride's Price. Arguing was no way to get her in a lovemaking mood.

"You're pretty quiet over there," he said finally. "You're making me nervous."

That got a smile out of her, albeit a small one. "It's been a busy day," she admitted. There was a vulnerable expression on her face he'd never seen before. Her eyes looked darker, kind of lost, as she added, "I feel so strange. Like I've changed completely. Like I'm not the same person at all."

"You aren't the same. You're an O'Malley now."

She grimaced, wrinkling her nose.

Annoyed by the gesture, Troy emphasized firmly, "You're *Ally O'Malley.*"

Her eyes widened as she stared at him, her faintly scornful expression erased by growing horror. She choked a little and covered her mouth. "Omigod!" she breathed through her fingers. "That sounds like a character in a nursery rhyme! Or a cartoon!"

"I like it."

"Well, I don't!" Her soft lips compressed into a determined line. "I'll simply go by my maiden name."

Troy frowned. "You'll go by O'Malley. And don't bother arguing," he ordered as she turned to him, clearly about to do so. "We're having a baby, and that baby will bear my last name, so it might as well be your last name, too."

Pul—leeze! Ally rolled her eyes, her faint melancholy replaced by annoyance. She'd escaped four bossy males and found another one. Well, after four, one shouldn't be hard to handle at all.

"Dream on, O'Malley." She tilted her hat over her eyes, and slouched in the seat, crossing her arms. "Feel free to name the baby we're not having whatever you want, but I'm keeping Cabrerra."

He slanted her a sardonic glance. "You can try. But you know everyone in Tangleweed will call you *Miz*—" he drawled the title

"—O'Malley, anyway. You'll just wear yourself out trying to correct them all the time. And draw even more attention to it."

He was right, Ally realized glumly. She narrowed her eyes, vowing stubbornly, "Well, as soon as this marriage ends, I'm going right back to Cabrerra. Which reminds me…" She held up her hand. "I hope you can return this ring when our marriage is over. It looks very expensive."

"Yeah, it's great what they can do with glass these days," Troy drawled, gripping the wheel to keep from strangling her. There she went again—being all stubborn and unreasonable and troublesome. Ever since they'd been married it had been one thing after another—starting with her determination to go stay at an isolated ranch and now this—talking about returning her ring when it hadn't been on her finger more than three hours.

"Troy…"

He looked over at her. She had a thoughtful expression on her face. What now? "Yeah?"

"You visited my aunt a lot, didn't you?"

Okay, he hadn't expected that question. He shrugged. "Every couple of months or so, whenever I wasn't traveling on the circuit."

"What did you two talk about? Besides Bride's Price, I mean."

We talked about you, Troy thought. *I told her how full of yourself you seemed; she told me you were just a loner, like she'd been as a girl.* He shrugged again. "This and that."

"Did she ever talk to you about Mick?"

"No. My grandfather was one topic we didn't discus." He slanted her a questioning glance. "What about you?"

"My aunt didn't really talk all that much with me. Not about anything really personal." Ally sounded regretful. "She was very reserved."

"Yeah, I got the impression she'd always been kind of shy."

Ally considered that, then slowly nodded.

Encouraged that she was finally listening, Troy added carefully, "But she seemed to enjoy my company. And I swear, she was prepared to sell Bride's Price to me."

He'd pushed too hard, too soon. Ally yawned and tilted her hat farther over her eyes. "Oh, I believe you," she said, her tone inferring the opposite. "It's just too bad for you and Mick she never got around to it."

His jaw tightening, Troy abandoned that fight to return to the initial issue. "Why do you suddenly want to go stay at Bride's Price so badly?"

She threw him a derisive glance. "There's nothing sudden about it. Why do you think I was so anxious for you to get that lease?"

He frowned. "I knew you wanted the money—didn't know you wanted to live out at the ranch. What are you going to do there? Raise cattle?"

"Maybe eventually," Ally conceded, "but primarily I want to concentrate on raising and training Peruvian Pasos."

"Pasos, huh? What's wrong with good old Texas quarter horses?" Troy asked—unknowingly echoing Ally's oldest brother.

Ally shook her head. Texan males—they were all the same. "I like Pasos. Have you ever ridden Misty's?"

"Nope. I've seen 'em, but I've never tried them out."

"Well, I have. Those gaited horses are wonderful to ride. So smooth and responsive. So easy. And Stan says their endurance is remarkable."

Troy's frown deepened at her rapt tone. She certainly sounded smitten with the breed. Which was fine; he didn't mind her raising horses, even Pasos. He just didn't want her to settle in too snugly at Bride's Price. He needed that deed to seal the deal with Mick about managing the Running M.

He said casually, "Well, if you want to raise Pasos, then I'll be glad to help you. Why don't you sell me Bride's Price? I'll give you top dollar and you can buy another place. One in better shape, nearer Austin, maybe—"

"Uh-uh." Ally shook her head, giving him a knowing glance. "No way, no how. I love Bride's Price, and besides, I'd feel like I was betraying Aunt Eileen if I sold it to your family, after she managed to hold out against Mick for all those years."

Troy didn't like hearing that at all. He was tempted to argue with her, to tell her again her aunt had been ready to sell—well, almost ready to sell. But he reached the turnoff to the ranch right then, so he decided to wait. The way he figured it, he'd have plenty of time alone with Ally to change her way of thinking.

They pulled up in front of the house fifteen minutes later. Troy had been there often during the past year, and at first glance, nothing seemed changed from the last time Eileen Hennessey had waved goodbye from her front porch. In the light of the setting sun the white paint glowed softly. The branches of the massive oak that sheltered the house swayed gently in the warm breeze.

But after he retrieved his duffel bag and one of her boxes from the truck and followed Ally in through the front door, Troy glanced around in surprise. "This looks different," he said, setting his bag and her box in the small living room which Eileen had always referred to as her front parlor. "Last time I was here, Eileen had this place so crammed with knickknacks and thing-amabobs a man could hardly move."

Now the room was almost empty, with just the overstuffed sofa and a couple of neatly stacked boxes remaining. "What did you do with everything?" He glanced at the boxes, lifting his brows. "Is it all in there?"

Ally shook her head. "Those are my books. I brought them over a couple days ago. I kept Aunt Eileen's dishes, quilts, personal journals and letters, but gave most of her china statues and a bunch of paperbacks and magazines I found in the second floor bedroom to the church for their fall rummage sale." Ally had been surprised to find all those love stories from the thirties and forties packed neatly away upstairs in an old trunk. Janie, who was in charge of the rummage sale again this year, had been thrilled with the china figurines, and even more so with the vintage romances. They'd sell really well, she'd assured Ally.

Troy followed Ally through the house to see what other changes she'd made. Like the Cabrerra place, the little ranch house was constructed of thick limestone walls. The fireplace had been built smack-dab in the middle of the downstairs with the big hearth opening unto the front room. All the other downstairs rooms—the kitchen, dining room, bathroom and a bedroom— circled the central fireplace. The second floor was reached by a set of stairs next to the fireplace wall.

"There's not much up there," Ally said as Troy eyed the narrow, steep steps consideringly. "Just a couple of old trunks I haven't had the chance to go through yet, and a rope-strung spool bed."

Except for the kitchen and upstairs, Ally had removed the old pictures from the walls and packed whatever furniture she could move into the old shed that had served as a garage until Eileen could no longer drive. In the downstairs bedroom, she'd taken apart the antique bed, leaning the thick mattress and the scrolled white iron headboard against the wall to make room to paint.

The house definitely needed cosmetic work, and the plumbing— judging by the leaking faucet in the kitchen—had issues. But Carlos Cabrerra had always ensured the house stayed sound for his wife's aunt, and his sons had done the same after he died.

Ally wondered what Troy thought of it all. He didn't say much during the short tour, but after they'd retrieved the rest of their stuff from the truck and were standing in the front room once more, he admitted, "You've done a lot here."

Ally felt a little glow of pleasure. "I've been coming over whenever I could spare an hour or two, but now that I'll actually be living here, I hope to make progress a lot faster, not just with the house, but with the stables and corrals, as well."

"Makes sense." He glanced toward the bedroom they'd just walked through. "But I see you broke down the bed…."

"I wanted it out of the way while I painted. There's a twin bed up in the attic, and a daybed out on the back screened porch. So," she said brightly, anxious to get off the subject of beds. "Are you hungry?"

"I could eat," he acknowledged, and gave her a slow grin. "I can just about always eat. The big question is, can you cook?"

"I can't remember a time I didn't know how to cook," Ally replied, and got to work.

Although the meal she rustled up was just chicken fried steak with fresh green beans, mashed potatoes and gravy, Troy ate like he'd never tasted anything so good, taking seconds of potatoes, and thirds of the steak.

"You sure can cook, Ally O'Malley," he told her, his eyes half closed as he savored a bite.

"Cabrerra," she corrected him, provoked by the name but secretly pleased by the compliment.

Troy raised a brow and, chewing his steak, let it pass.

Ally took her time eating and cleaning up, as well, but still the evening seemed to fly by as she washed the dishes. Troy did the drying, picking up the towel without her having to ask, listening to her as she talked. As the shadows outside the kitchen window were swallowed by the darkness, Troy grew uncharacteristically quieter, while Ally became uncharacteristically chattier, discussing how she planned to fix the corrals and build a chicken coop. How she wanted to start a fall garden, and was determined to save enough from the money he gave her to buy a couple of Peruvian Paso mares by the end of the year.

Finally, Ally lapsed into silence, unable to think of one more thing to talk about. Nervously, she emptied the sink, and wrung out the washcloth. She draped it over the leaky faucet, giving Troy a sidelong glance as he finished drying the last pan.

His rugged face was solemn, his eyes hidden by his lowered lashes. He gave the pan one last swipe, then set it in the cupboard before he turned to face her.

Ally's breath caught at the look in his eyes.

"So," he said, tossing his dish towel on the counter. "It's getting dark. Maybe we'd better decide where we're going to sleep."

Chapter Eight

"If conception remains elusive, reevaluate the heifer's disposition. Is she skittish? Or possibly obdurate about accepting the male?"
—*Successful Breeding: A Guide for the Cattleman*

Oh, how Ally wanted to believe that Troy was simply tired, anxious to turn in after what had been—for her, at least—a long and emotionally exhausting day. But one look at his expression made that hope evaporate quicker than a snowflake in the Chihuahuan Desert. Hot, unmistakable desire burned in his heavy-lidded gaze.

Uh-oh. Another thing they should have talked about. Ally turned and picked up the dish towel he'd discarded, folding it neatly to avoid his gaze. He obviously wanted to make love. She really, really didn't. Okay, maybe her *body* really, really *did,* but her mind knew it was a bad idea. Been there, done that (almost, anyway). And what had she gotten for it? Anger, pain, embarrassment—and Troy's imaginary baby.

An imaginary baby and an imaginary marriage to an all-too-real man. A man who imagined they'd made love before, and was eager to do so again.

Ally hung up the folded towel and met his eyes. It was still there; that hot, intent look. She gnawed on her lower lip—then wished she hadn't when Troy's hungry gaze fastened on her mouth.

"Then again, who wants to sleep?" he asked huskily, and took a step toward her.

Ally took a step back, holding up her hand. "Wait a minute, Troy. We need to talk about this."

"What's there to talk about?" He took another step toward her. "We're married."

"We married so I could get control of Bride's Price, remember? And you said all you wanted was that lease."

"Yeah, well…" Catching her hand, he reeled her in, locking his arm around her waist. "What I want now is you."

He covered her mouth with his. His lips were warm—and so gentle that Ally's mouth softened in involuntary response. She pressed closer against his hard chest, and he slanted his head to kiss her more deeply. His lips firmed, turned possessive. He drew on her mouth, stealing her breath. And—just like at the wedding—Ally's thoughts began to blur.

He smelled so good, like expensive cologne and dish soap. The slight stubble on his chin felt rough and exciting against her skin. Her breasts flattened against his chest, and her knees weakened. She clutched his shoulders with trembling fingers, trying not to fall.

His arm tightened around her waist, then loosened. Slowly he broke the kiss and lifted his head. His eyes were so dark only a thin rim of green remained around his pupil. He lowered his head and nipped her bottom lip, right in the center.

Ally moaned as the tingling pain shot from her mouth to her nipples, making them peak. Gasping, she wrenched herself away.

She leaned against the counter and covered her flushed cheeks. She just couldn't think straight when he touched her. Something in her brain short-circuited, scattering logical thought completely.

He reached for her.

She sidestepped, avoiding his big, clever hands. "Troy—stop," she said huskily.

"Stop?" He repeated the word as if he'd never heard it before—and he probably hadn't in this kind of situation. Heaven knew she hadn't used it in that motel room.

She shook her head, said desperately, "We can't do this—"

"Sure we can."

"No, we can't." She moved back a step. "You haven't forgotten, have you, what happened the last time we started…all this."

"We ended up in bed together."

"Exactly."

He'd proved her point, but Troy still didn't get the message. He moved closer. "Yeah, that's exactly where I want to be. In bed again. With you."

The husky note in his voice, the yearning in his heavy-lidded gaze made her breath catch, her heart gallop. She wanted to give in so bad, and that was the problem. It was too risky, too scary. If he touched her again…

"It's dangerous," she blurted out.

Troy stopped in his tracks, his arm falling to his side. He stared at her. "Dangerous?" he repeated. "To the baby?"

Ally returned his gaze uncertainly, not sure what to do. She didn't want to outright lie; this whole situation was already complicated enough. She needed more time to think, really think, this whole thing through. Yet Troy—judging by his tensed muscles and the restless desire in his eyes—was obviously stuck on action mode.

"You think making love would be dangerous for the baby?" he repeated sharply.

"Or for me," she prevaricated.

He ran his hand through his hair, concern and frustration flickering across his rugged face. "What makes you think so? I thought you said you haven't been to a doctor."

"I haven't. But I—I read about it. In a book."

"What book?"

"You know—that famous one Oprah recommends. *What to Expect When You're Expecting to Expect.*"

He frowned. "I think I've heard of it. Kind of a mouthful, though."

"But catchy, don't you think? Oprah liked it—and who can argue with Oprah?" Not giving him time to answer, she hurried on, "The doctor who wrote it—Dr. Spock—"

His brows rose. "The guy on *Star Trek?*"

"Did I say Spock? I meant Spunk. Dr. Spunk. She's a woman and the leading authority on the subject of sex and pregnant women." Heavens, Ally thought, resisting the urge to wring her hands. She was so bad at this!

But he bought the lie, just not the details. His brows lowered in a frown again, and he planted his hands on his hips. "Are you sure you read the book right?"

"Positive."

"It said no sexual intercourse."

"None."

"What about…" He eyed her consideringly. "Other things. Like—"

"Nothing—nothing at all," Ally interrupted hurriedly, before he could enumerate the "other things" he had in mind. "All contact—any contact at all—is strictly prohibited. Even kissing," she added for good measure.

"Kissing?" He was definitely looking skeptical again. "How could that hurt?"

"Apparently it stirs up a pregnant woman's hormones, which is risky. So Dr. Spock—"

"Spunk."

"Spunk—recommends complete abstention."

"Oh, yeah?" His frown deepened into a scowl. "For how long?"

"It varies," Ally said vaguely.

Vague wasn't good enough for Troy. "Let's check it out." He glanced around. "Where's the book?"

Ally glanced around, too—as if the mythical book might somehow appear in the empty kitchen. "Hmm, now, where did I put it? Let me see…"

But Troy wasn't waiting for her to find it. He strode into the living room and over to the boxes she'd brought. "Is it in here?" Opening the top one, he began to search for himself.

"Um, maybe."

He started digging, emptying out the carton. Ally watched without saying a word of discouragement—it was good for him to stay busy—as he pulled out her precious books on equine and cattle care, followed by her *EQUUS* magazines, and even her vintage *Dragonlance* paperbacks and stacked them all on the floor.

Troy was too intent on his search to make conversation, only commenting, "I've got this one, too—it's good," when he pulled out her hefty *Successful Breeding: A Guide for the Cattleman.* Ally remained quiet, as well. It wasn't until he finished digging through her second box, uncovering more horse books and novels but not— *surprise! surprise!*—Dr. Spunk's epistle, that she finally spoke up.

"Darn it. I must've left it at the Circle C," she said with a sigh, and feigned regret. "But I'm positive Dr. Spunk said to avoid sexual activities, and to be honest—" *oh, let's be honest here, Ally, at least a little* "—I really, really don't want to take any chances."

That last part was the absolute truth. And either her sincerity came through or Troy recognized how miserable she felt, because he finally backed off.

Still crouched beside the now empty boxes, his taut expression softened as he studied her face. "You want to wait."

"Yes."

"For how long?" When she hesitated to answer, he prompted, "Until you see a doctor?"

Since she had no intentions of ever seeing a doctor, that sounded reasonable. Ally nodded, relieved by the suggestion.

Troy didn't look relieved in the least. He looked tense and frustrated, and his voice was grim when he said, "Okay, if you're worried, then we'll wait. Until you see a doctor and you're sure it's safe."

Ally had plenty of time to think later that night. Troy, looking disgruntled, opted to sleep on the back screened-in porch, so she immediately scuttled upstairs to the attic bedroom, anxious to get out of harm's—and temptation's—way.

She put on her nightgown and turned out the small light, but sleep remained elusive. Moonlight seeped past the big oak and through the small window at the end of the peaked-ceiling room, but what kept Ally awake were the memories of all that had happened that day. Images kept tumbling through her mind. Of the pretty dress Misty had lent her. The clerk's starry-eyed look. Linc offering his car, Cole's hard expression. And all her brothers walking away.

That memory hurt, so she concentrated on her big problem. The problem that stood about six feet tall, had a teasing white grin and *I'm-gonna-getcha* green eyes.

Troy Michael O'Malley.

One thing was for sure, she decided, laying her hands on top of the covers and twisting her wedding ring. The inclination she'd felt earlier in the day to *make* Troy realize she truly wasn't pregnant was gone completely. Since the imaginary baby was the only thing keeping him from jumping her bones, she'd simply keep playing make-believe awhile. Because if she hadn't been (supposedly) pregnant, she had no doubts at all she'd be down on that porch making love with Troy at that very minute.

The thought made her toes curl. She lifted her hand to touch her swollen mouth…then resolutely straightened her toes and dropped her hand back on the covers, tugging the sheet up under her chin.

It would be stupid—totally stupid—to get sexually involved with Troy. This marriage was a temporary arrangement, nothing more than a business deal. And everyone knew that mixing business with pleasure was never a good idea.

She sighed. Even if it wasn't, she just wasn't cut out for a passing affair. Blame it on her conservative upbringing. Blame it on watching her brothers' inability to commit to the women they dated, and probably slept with. Blame it on the fact that— having waited twenty-four years already to get involved with a man—she didn't want to settle for anything less than a "forever" kind of relationship.

And Troy wasn't a forever kind of man.

She wanted love, she thought, staring at the swaying leaf shadows chasing across the peaked ceiling. The kind of love her parents had shared. The kind that—years after he'd lost her—had made her father's hard face soften whenever he talked about his wife. Ally wanted that, too, and lots of babies—real babies—as well.

But that wasn't going to happen with Troy. Bull riders lived their lives eight seconds at a time. Short and sweet and exciting— that was the kind of relationships men like Troy sought; the kind he wanted with her. He certainly didn't love her. Not that she loved him, either, she reassured herself. What she felt—her attraction to him—wasn't anything more than simple physical desire. Lust in its rawest, most basic form. Regrettable and misplaced, certainly, but perfectly understandable. Troy was an attractive man. But just *physically* attractive, she assured herself firmly. She wasn't drawn to him mentally or emotionally—she was just drawn to his glinting green eyes, square jaw and wide mouth, and (okay, she admitted it) totally ripped, muscled body.

Even if he did fall in love with her (which was not gonna happen) and she fell in love with him (no way, no how was she doing that!), it still would never work. Most people might believe Romeo and Juliet had been a great love story, but Ally knew better. Shakespeare had been providing a grim warning about marrying someone your family didn't like, which—even if it didn't end in murder or suicide—was certain to cause unnecessary pain all around. Oh, the twins and Kyle might come around at some point, but neither Cole nor Old Mick ever would. She hated being estranged from her family, and other than a few distant cousins, Old Mick was the only family Troy had left.

Yes, she had several good reasons for staying pregnant, so to speak. For not convincing Troy of the truth quite yet. But the reason that bucked past the buzzer and outscored them all, was the reason she discovered the next day, during their first morning together at Bride's Price.

Troy didn't say much to her when she came downstairs. Definitely not a morning person, Ally decided, checking out his whiskery chin, rumpled hair and his grumpy expression from the corner of her eye as she strode past him in the living room. She left him alone, and he joined her in the kitchen as the coffee finished perking, his damp hair and shaven chin proof that he'd showered while she made breakfast.

After they finished the eggs she prepared, Troy wandered outside while Ally retrieved a collection of paint cans from the back porch and carried them into the downstairs bedroom and set them on the floor. She'd crouched down to pry open the first can when—voilà! Troy reappeared at her side like a bad-tempered genie in jeans, to remove the screwdriver she was using from her hand.

"What do you think you're doing?" he demanded, squatting beside her.

Ally bit back a sarcastic "picking daisies" to go with a simpler answer that even a man could understand. "I'm getting ready to paint."

"No, you're not. You're pregnant. Even if painting wasn't too physically taxing for a pregnant woman, which even an idiot—" *like you* remained unsaid "—should realize it is, the fumes can't be good for the baby. And—" he scowled at the ladder she'd propped against the wall "—you're definitely not going up on that thing and taking a chance on falling."

By the time he paused to take a breath, Ally's anger had reached boiling point. She was just about to tell him what he could do with his unwanted advice when he added the magic words: "If you want this damn room painted, then I'll paint it for you."

Ally shut her mouth. Despite his earlier implication, she definitely wasn't an idiot. Nor was painting her favorite chore. She hesitated a second, then said dulcetly, "I can't let you do that…."

"I want to!" he snarled, and glanced impatiently at the cans. "Which one are you using?"

"I haven't decided yet. Virgil at the hardware told me I could return the cans I don't use." She deftly stole back her screwdriver and quickly popped open the lids to reveal the paint inside.

Troy took one glance and shook his head. "You're kidding right? Pink, pink, pink and more pink? What's to choose?"

"C'mon, Troy. Even an idiot—" *like you* remained unsaid "—

can see they're all different." She pointed to the brightest shade, a cotton candy color. "This one is called Possibly Pink."

Troy raised his eyebrows. "Someone had doubts?"

"This one is Pink Wink."

"Sounds like a sty," Troy decided. He glanced at it disparagingly. "Yep, it's pink eye, all right."

"This one is my favorite. It's called Pink Destiny. It's so light, so airy— What are you snorting about?" she demanded. "What's wrong with it?"

"What's wrong? I'll tell you what's wrong. It's a damn stupid name. Pink Destiny." He made a disgusted sound. "What's that supposed to mean, anyway? Pretentious Pink is what they should've called it."

Ally gritted her teeth. "Quit it. You're not supposed to choose by the name, but by the color."

"Well, why did they name them, then? Why not just call them pink one, pink two, pink three and pink four?"

Ally had no answer for that, and she was tired of arguing about it. "Look, just because you don't like pink—"

"I like pink!" he declared. "Who says I don't? I like *that* color just fine," he added, pointing to the last choice. "What's it called?"

"Berry Pink," Ally said grudgingly. She added suspiciously, "Why do you like it?"

He glanced from the paint can to her face. His eyes glinted wickedly. "Because it's the same color as your cheeks whenever you blush."

Ally tried to fight it, but she could feel her face heating.

Troy's mouth curved slowly into a satisfied smile. "There ya go. Berry Pink, all right. I vote for that one."

Ally said with dignity, "I'm not sure—"

"Trust me. You'll like it. Now, go on—" he urged when she

just stood there "—go get some fresh air. I'll let you know when I'm done."

That sounded like a fine idea to Ally. She grabbed a pen and pocket-size notebook from one of the boxes in the front room and escaped outside.

For a while, she wandered around the crumbling stable and broken corral, making a list of the supplies and tools she'd need to repair them. Finally, however, it grew too hot to be out in the sun so she headed to the hammock hanging from a bigtooth maple at the edge of the woods.

Reaching it, Ally kicked off her sandals and climbed onto the soft cotton web and lay down, relieved to escape the worst of the heat as she continued working on her to-do list. But soon, the past weeks of stress and her long sleepless night caught up with her. Lulled by soft dappled shade and the gentle swaying of the hammock, she let her pen and paper fall against her stomach, and her eyes drifted shut. Just for a little while.

A slight jarring of the hammock woke her. Ally drowsily lifted her lashes to find Troy standing next to her, his tall figure blocking her view of the fluttering green leaves overhead. She blinked, lifting a hand to her eyes and trying to focus as her sleepy gaze wandered over him.

He looked…hot. In more ways than one. In deference to the brain-baking midday sun, he had his hat on but had removed his shirt. His wide, tanned shoulders glistened with sweat, and his broad, muscular chest was adorned here and there with pink paint—a liberal swipe across one well-defined pec; random flecks to decorate his rib cage and washboard abdomen. He'd even gotten paint on his Wranglers, she noted absently, as her gaze drifted lower. On the waistband and along the buttoned ridge of—

Suddenly realizing where her eyes lingered, her gaze flickered up to his face.

He was watching her. Despite the ninety-plus temperature, she shivered at his expression. A war paint slash of Berry Pink across his cheek highlighted the hot, green glint in his eyes as he stared at her. They burned her, those eyes. Sparked an answering heat in her belly. So she avoided them by studying the light bump in his masculine nose, the square lines of his jaw, the sturdy strength of his neck, before fastening her gaze on his mouth. Yeah, as she noted before, he had a great mouth. A little wide, maybe, but with nicely shaped lips and straight white teeth.

He was so sexy, she thought, with almost dreamy despair. How could he look so good and be such a dirty dog?

Then his lips moved and he spoke. For a moment, Ally thought she'd misheard…but then the words sank in. Her breath caught and her heart leaped. She realized she'd been doing him an injustice. Troy O'Malley might be a womanizer, a drinker and a liar. A terrible tease and too quick with his fists.

But he certainly wasn't all bad. In fact, Ally decided, he might be the most wonderful man she'd ever met.

"What did you say?" she asked faintly—just for the sheer joy of hearing again, the question she'd thought no man would ever ask her.

"I said," he growled, glaring down at her impatiently, "what do you want me to do now?"

Chapter Nine

"If conception *still* remains elusive, reevaluate the male.
Is he too meek or aggressive in his pursuit of the female?"
—*Successful Breeding: A Guide for the Cattleman*

Ally wanted Troy to paint the other rooms a soft buttery cream. She wanted him to help move all the heavy furniture so she could polish the wooden floors. She wanted him to repair the leaky plumbing in the kitchen and fix the toilet in the bathroom.

Ally found plenty for Troy to do in the following days. Theirs was a match made in handyman heaven. He had the brawn, and she had the brains to use his brawn to her best advantage. Whatever she requested, Troy did without complaint.

Ally worked alongside him, ignoring his protests for the most part. It just wasn't in her nature to be idle all day. But when he stubbornly insisted on doing the heavy lifting and all the painting himself, she graciously acquiesced. Playing pregnant definitely had its advantages, Ally decided.

When they had the house under control, they immediately started work repairing the corrals near the old barn and stable. Troy took the time to put up a gym bar in the stables, and had a pummel horse delivered from the Running M as well. The equipment, Ally knew, helped maintain and build the upper body strength and balance so necessary to a bull rider's success.

She never watched him work out. When he headed into the barn each afternoon, she'd head into the house to make dinner. Cooking for two, she discovered, didn't seem nearly the chore cooking for five did, especially since Troy was so appreciative of her efforts. But not as appreciative as she was of all he managed to accomplish. By the end of the week, Ally was almost giddy about the progress they'd made at Bride's Price. The house was clean, painted and livable. The leaky plumbing had been fixed, and outside near the kitchen, they'd broken ground for a fall garden. Most important, the corral near the barn was repaired and ready for stock, and the stables and barn would be usable weeks sooner than she'd hoped for.

Anything she wanted done, Troy did. In fact, there was only one downside in Ally's DIY paradise. The thing she wanted most of all…was Troy.

And he wanted her, too. While she did her best to hide her growing desire, he didn't bother to hide his at all. He never touched her—with his hands, anyway. But Ally would look up from doing the dishes, or sweeping the floor, or whacking nails into a post to find him watching. His eyes were on her constantly, often crinkled with amusement or needling mischief; occasionally thoughtful or impatient in response to their conversation. But always present deep in his green gaze was a proprietary gleam, an awareness that she was female and (albeit temporarily) his wife.

That darn sexy look never failed to make her breath catch, and her muscles tense. It made her stop what she was doing and forget what she was saying. It filled her head with memories of being in his arms, memories of how his callused hands had felt stroking her smooth skin.

All that wanting and remembering kept building as each day passed, thickening and heating the air between them like the summer storm gathering over the hills. And if the days were bad working outside together on the corrals and stable, the evenings were worse.

No one bothered the "honeymooners;" no one called. Troy and Ally seemed very much alone, penned up together in the little house on the isolated ranch. Distractions were limited once the sun went down. The television was tiny and reception unpredictable. Eileen had a DVD player, but the only DVDs they could find were ones they'd seen a million times.

So it became a ritual in the evenings after the mosquitoes chased them inside to sit on the overstuffed chintz couch in the small front room, with Aunt Eileen's old-fashioned oil lamp casting a softly flickering glow over the freshly painted cream walls. They did a lot of talking to fill up the shadowy darkness. Ally talked about her parents and her brothers; about how Linc loved old cars, Luke loved horses and how Kyle, despite his tough-guy exterior, was a sucker for anyone in need. She didn't talk about Cole, though. Although he hid it better than her oldest brother did, Ally could tell that Troy disliked Cole, possibly as much as Cole disliked him. Because Troy loved Misty? Ally wondered.

Troy told Ally about growing up alone—just him and his mom after his father died. How he'd hated leaving their small ranch at first when his grandfather insisted they live with him on the Running M, and how he'd hated even more going away to the prestigious boarding school back East that Mick had insisted he attend, in hopes Troy'd make contacts for the political career Mick had planned for him.

Yet, despite Mick's maneuvering, Troy knew politics wasn't in his future. Ranching and bull riding, Troy told Ally, were in his blood.

Ally could tell by the way he talked that, like most bull riders, Troy was addicted to the "eight second" adrenaline high of the extreme sport, but that Running M had a hold on his heart, as well. When Troy inadvertently let slip that he—and not Mick— had bought the computer for the library, and "invested" in various struggling businesses in town, she realized that Troy also cared deeply about his hometown of Tangleweed.

"No wonder you didn't get banned along with the twins from the bar," she exclaimed. "Big Bob owes you."

"He doesn't owe me, exactly. He pays me what he can each month and sometimes I take part of that payment in beer." He grinned. "Saves on paperwork and trips to the bank and all."

"I bet," Ally said dryly, but frowned a little over what he'd told her. "I didn't know Big Bob's or the No-Tell Motel was in trouble." She studied the chiseled angles of his cheeks and de- termined jut of his chin revealed by lamplight as she sat facing him from "her" end of the couch.

Sprawled out at "his" end, Troy grimaced. "No reason you should know, and—" he sent her a warning look "—I'd appre- ciate it if you didn't spread it around. I wouldn't want Big Bob or Elmer Jerome to feel bad—not that they should. Lots of people are struggling in this economy."

Including the Cabrerra clan, Ally thought. She pointed out, "But if the motel and bar have become part of the O'Malley holdings, people are bound to know. I can't see Mick keeping it quiet." When Mick gave, whether it was a donation to the town or the church, he made sure *everyone* knew about it and was appropriately grateful.

"The company didn't invest in them. I did, with the money I inherited from my mother's family. Mick doesn't know," Troy said shortly.

"You used your personal fortune, and not O'Malley money?" Ally asked in surprise. Like many ranching families, the O'Malley holdings had been incorporated decades earlier. Ally knew that members of the family—like his second cousins on Troy's grandmother's side—held stock in O'Malley, Inc., with Mick holding the largest controlling block.

"I get it," she said slowly. "You couldn't convince Mick to help them out, could you?" Because despite his talk of investing, she knew that's what Troy had actually done: helped out the Tangleweed businesses.

"Mick would have done it," Troy said in defense of his grandfather. "The only thing is…" He hesitated, trying to find the right way to say it. "Mick tends to want to be in control. Sometimes he can take over a bit."

"Sometimes? A bit?" Ally repeated dryly. "Your grandfather always has to be top dog, whether it's serving on the Meyer County Cattleman's Association, or the town council." She thought it over, then said in a musing tone, "I think that's why he's so fixated on Bride's Price."

Troy sat up a little straighter. "What do you mean? The reason Mick wants Bride's Price back is because it's a beautiful little ranch—the land he inherited from his father. He loves it."

"Seems to me, it's not love of the land that's driving him. I think your grandfather becomes obsessed with what he can't have or control, and Bride's Price is a perfect example. He doesn't need Bride's Price. When he cheated on Aunt Eileen and married Margaret Meyer, he got the Running M—the largest spread in Meyer County. Which was probably the reason he went after Margaret."

Troy wanted to dispute her conclusion, but he couldn't. Mick had never shown much affection toward his wife, or grieved long when she died. And Troy knew for a fact that he'd pushed his own son—Troy's father Patrick—into an advantageous marriage, as well. Troy's mother, Grace, had admitted as much, right before she died.

But Mick was Troy's grandfather; the man who'd stood in place of his father for most of Troy's life. Mick had put Troy up on the back of his first pony. He'd inadvertently sparked Troy's love of bull riding when he'd entered him in the mutton-busting event at the county fair when he was four. He'd taught Troy all he knew about ranching, and how to make a profit at the often precarious enterprise. He'd turned over the controlling shares so Troy could take charge of the Running M.

No, he and Mick didn't always see eye to eye, but Mick was family, and Troy didn't like hearing Ally put down one of his own.

His eyes narrowed on her faintly disdainful expression. "People marry for a variety of reasons."

"Not Cabrerras," Ally stated proudly. "In my family, people only marry for love."

"You didn't."

Ally gasped, the blunt statement hitting her like a blow.

Troy pushed on. "You married so you could gain something—basically, my money—and get control of Bride's Price. How's that different from what Mick may have done?"

"It is different," she protested. "You wanted that lease. You got something in return."

"Who's to say my grandmother didn't get something in return, too?"

"Okay, maybe she did," Ally admitted, after a pause. "But that's different. This isn't a real marriage—"

"It damn well is a real marriage. It's as legal and binding as any other."

"It's temporary. A marriage of convenience."

"Well, I'm not finding it very convenient," Troy told her. "I'm finding it damn frustrating. In my opinion, it's time for me to re-assemble that damn double bed in that damn pink bedroom so we can sleep together the way we damn well *should* have been doing all along."

She didn't answer, and his lips thinned. "Have you even made a doctor's appointment yet?"

"You know I haven't."

He eyed her grimly. "All I know is you better do it soon and find out where we stand. Because I can't go on like this much longer."

And getting up from the couch, he strode from the room.

The small argument stoked the tension even higher. The next day—their ninth on the ranch—the air seemed to crackle between them. It didn't help that the storm gathering over the hills hadn't ripened to rain yet. Ally knew it might not; that it might pass their small piece of Texas without providing a drop of moisture. She was tired of the suffocating humidity and wanted the gray clouds to shed rain or move on. But they hovered stubbornly overhead, making the air heavy and oppressive, like a weight bearing down.

As the evening darkened, the air grew even thicker, Troy more curt and surly. Afraid to say the wrong thing and set him off, Ally picked up *Successful Breeding* to read after dinner, holding the dense tome like a barrier as she sat at her end of the couch.

The air in the little ranch house felt stifling. Even opening all the windows and turning on all the fans hadn't helped. Sitting there trying to read, Ally strove to appear calm when all she wanted to do was writhe in the heat—heat from the weather, heat from Troy's brooding green gaze that she could feel burning through the brown binding of the book she held. He didn't even pretend to be watching the fuzzy show on the television. He just kept staring her way.

She turned the page. Her fingertips stuck to the corner, and the paper rustled noisily in the quiet. Perspiration dampened her temples. She brushed the moisture away, ignoring Troy's brooding gaze as it followed her movements.

She tried to focus on her book, but couldn't. She stared at it, anyway—the print blurring as she fought not to look at Troy as the heat inside her built higher and higher with every passing moment. Her fingers trembled. She clutched the book tighter, resisting the urge to fling it away—to escape outside. To run wild and crazy beneath the dark clouds like she and her brothers had once done as kids, all five of them, whooping and galloping and racing around the yard with their arms spread wide—high on the energy that made their skin tingle and their hair stand on end. They'd kept running, not stopping until Carlos Cabrerra stepped out on the porch, his angry face lit by the lightning. "Get in here!" he'd roared, louder than the thunder booming overhead. "You kids know better! Do you want to get hit? It's dangerous out here!"

They'd fled inside to safety. But there was no safety in this little house tonight, Ally decided. If she stayed here, if she didn't move, passion would strike and burn her all up—

"Ally…"

She shot to her feet.

Troy jumped up, too, alarmed by her abrupt move. He stood facing her, eyes fixed on her face, hands flexing, muscles tensed and ready for action. "What?" he demanded, his gaze searching her face. "What's wrong?"

"Nothing's wrong," she told him. "You startled me…." She cleared her throat. "What did you want?"

He lifted an eyebrow. "I wondered if you wanted to play cards."

She didn't dare play anything with him. She needed to get out of there ASAP. "No, I can't. I need to go into town."

"Now?" He looked at her like she was crazy. *"Tonight?"*

She nodded.

"But why?"

To cool this situation down. "I need ice cream," she decided. "Mint chocolate chip."

He stared at her, apparently at a loss for words. "But it's almost seven," he said finally. He ran a hand through his hair. "The Piggly Wiggly will be closed soon."

"You're right. I'd better hurry." She glanced around, searching for the keys. Spotting them on the small table near the door, she went over and picked them up. "Can I use your truck?"

"No, you can't use my truck!" He snatched his keys away from her. "It's going to storm."

Ally didn't care. She wanted out now. Her eyes narrowed, and she put her hands on her hips. "I want ice cream."

"Fine. Then *I'll* go." Ignoring her protests, he sat on the couch and yanked on his boots. Standing up again, he stomped into the kitchen, reappeared moments later with the ice cooler and headed to the door. Grabbing his hat off the hook, he jammed it on his head.

"No, Troy, wait!" Still surprised, she tried to stop him, catching his arm as he yanked at the doorknob.

"Forget it. If you want ice cream, I'll get you ice cream," he barked, and slammed out.

Well! Ally blinked at the closed door. How had that happened? She'd just wanted to get away; she'd never meant for him to go.

Ally felt bad about that. She felt worse when it started to rain, and even more so when Troy finally arrived home four hours later with his hat and clothes soaked, his boots caked with mud up past the ankles.

"What happened?" she asked.

"Tire blew halfway home," he said. "And the shoulder of the highway was one big mud puddle."

Ally felt guilty, all right. But she was totally appalled when he opened the cooler he'd lugged in and she discovered he'd gone "baby shopping."

"I saw the monitor in the window of the hardware store and figured I might as well pick it up, since it would be handy to have now," he told her, toweling off his hair as she examined the device. "This one has an extra-long range so we can set it up in the pink bedroom, and rig it so we can hear it not only in the living room, but in the stables, as well."

"Troy…"Ally regarded it helplessly. "You shouldn't have bought this…."

"I wanted to. And I couldn't resist these little guys, either." He pulled out not one, not two, but three stuffed horses—a black one, a little pinto and a coffee-colored bay. "I figure this herd will do as a start, until you find some real stock for that stable."

Ally's chest felt tight. The stuffed horses were sweet with their soft fur, big brown eyes and floppy legs—but not as sweet as the cowboy watching her with a slight smile on his face, rain glistening on his hair and trailing down his lean cheek.

Somehow Ally found herself in his arms, her face buried against his broad shoulder, her arms clinging around his strong neck. She breathed in the fresh rain, leather-and-musky-man scent of him and admitted to herself that if Troy tried to make love with her right then—well, she wouldn't resist him at all.

But he didn't try, even though his arms tightened around her until she was crushed against his hard chest. He just gave her a quick hug and kissed the top of her head before setting her aside.

"Let's have some of that ice cream," he said huskily.

So that's what they did. Ate ice cream, and talked about the next day's work, then went off to bed. Separately. Just like always.

But for Ally something had changed. Playing pregnant was no longer much fun.

Make that no fun at all, she decided the next day, as she helped Troy install the baby monitor down at the stables—or rather, tried to help him in between phone call after phone call congratulating her and Troy on their "big" news. After the fifth call in less than an hour, Ally couldn't take it anymore.

"What did you say? Who did you talk to last night?" she asked Troy desperately, snapping her cell shut to escape Sue Ellen's coy questions. When it immediately started ringing again, Ally cautiously checked the caller ID and groaned.

"It's Emma Mae," she told Troy, "probably calling with an offer to print the news in the *Tumbleweed Times*."

"Nah," he said without looking up from the electrical wiring he was working on. "I told her it was too soon for that."

"What!" Ally turned the phone off completely and put it in her pocket, resisting the temptation to drown it in the water trough. To think, she'd fought with Cole to get the darned thing! "Did you tell the whole town?"

"Of course not. I didn't tell anyone. Except Emma Mae. Oh, and Virgil. He asked me who the monitor was for. And Dwayne Cronk asked about the horses while he was bagging them up at the Pig Wig. But that's it. And I told them all not to spread the news around—that it was early days yet."

"Well, that worked," Ally said in dry despair.

She kept her phone off for the rest of the day, but it didn't matter—her discomfort about playing pregnant had escalated into apprehension. Every call of congratulations had made her feel more like a fraud and would, she feared, make Troy feel more of a fool once the truth was revealed.

Preoccupied with her own thoughts, she didn't say much as they did dishes after dinner while Troy talked about finishing the fencing on the north range, anxious to get the job done so he could finally move his cattle over from the Running M.

Ally had learned during the time they'd spent together that the cattle he had leased the land for were special; that he'd developed the herd himself, concentrating on developing a leaner, healthier breed of beef. She knew Mick, impatient with his grandson's efforts, wanted to blend the animals in with the other stock, and that Troy was determined not to let that happen. Knowing Troy like she now did, Ally thought as she absently swished a red plate through the suds, she would bet her last dime those cattle would be grazing on Bride's Price grass by the end of the week.

Yes, she'd learned a lot about Troy since their hasty marriage, she realized, rinsing a glass in hot water and handing it to him to be dried. She'd learned his seemingly sunny, easygoing nature hid an unrelenting determination to have his own way. That he played hard, but worked harder. That he thrived on challenges, the bigger the better. That he was slow to anger and quick to tease.

She'd always known that he was the most irritating, exasperating, annoying man she'd ever met; albeit the sexiest and best kisser, as well. Now she knew without a doubt that despite his carefree ways, when it came to family—*his* family—Troy O'Malley cared deeply.

She couldn't do it any longer. Use the possibility of a baby to keep him in line. But before she told him the truth, she needed to talk to a lawyer. She'd jumped into this marriage to get Bride's Price, but she hadn't been very smart about it. She hadn't checked out the legalities of the situation, and it was past time she did. What if, once he realized there really was no baby, Troy became so angry he backed out of their deal? What would happen if he wanted to divorce immediately? Would she have to relinquish control of Bride's Price to Cole?

"I'd like to go into Austin tomorrow," she said. "Can I use the truck?"

"Sure."

"I'll probably leave here about ten." She pulled the plug in the sink and dried off her hands, secretly admiring, as she always did, her sparkling ring. "I'll pick up more supplies while I'm there for the fencing."

He gave her a questioning glance. "Do you need me to go with you?"

"No, but thanks. I just want to run a few errands."

He cocked his head, and from the quizzical look in his eyes, Ally suspected he wanted to ask if one of those errands was seeing a doctor. But he didn't ask, and she didn't mention that it was a lawyer, and not a doctor, that she planned to visit.

He'd know soon enough, Ally thought sadly, that the baby he was obviously so excited about, simply didn't exist.

By the time Ally left for Austin the next morning, Troy was already hard at work on the worn barn, prying off rotting boards to be replaced. Midmornings were the best time of the day to work, he decided a couple of hours later, as he paused to take a break. The sun was hot enough to make him sweat, but wasn't unbearable as it would be later in the day.

He wiped the sweat from his face, mentally debating whether to go get a drink of water. Usually when they were working, Ally would break away about this time to make ice tea or lemonade to have with a snack. He missed that today— he missed *her*, he realized. He'd gotten used to being with her; the place seemed too quiet without her around. Not that she talked all that much when they worked. She just got right down to it, whatever the job might be. She was different from the other women he knew; more interested in horses, ranching and keeping house than clubbing and designer clothes. Her short nails were always clean, but her slender hands were callused.

He liked that about her. Admired how hard, how intently she worked, whether she was shooting staples in the fence or cleaning her aunt's old house.

But it worried him, too. It was strange, he reflected, to have someone to worry about. He'd never had to take care of anyone before, to watch out for their welfare and well-being, which—in Ally's case—mostly involved making sure that she didn't do too much. She needed to slow down if she didn't want to end up hurting herself or the baby.

He needed to get this chore done before she got back, he decided. She'd want to help if he was still going at it, and she'd looked tired when she left this morning.

Hefting his crowbar, he returned to the job at hand, enjoying the pull on his muscles as he worked, planning out what else needed to be done in the following days. Although he still intended to convince Ally to give up Bride's Price, to find some other place to raise those horses she was dreaming about, it simply made sense to fix up these old stables, the neglected fences and land. The way he figured it, the more improvements he made now, the fewer would have to be done later.

Still, it would be a shame to turn the little property into the hunting reserve Mick had mentioned. Maybe he could talk the old man out of it, Troy thought, flinging a piece of splintered board on his growing pile of scrap.

He'd finished with the barn and moved on to yanking rusty nails out of the corral posts near the stable door when he caught sight of Misty's red roadster barreling up the road toward the house.

She must have seen him, too, because the little car changed direction, swooping around to bump across the ragged grass until, running out of level terrain, it pulled to a stop at the top of the path.

Troy dropped his hammer and started toward her. "Hey, kiddo!" he called as she opened her car door.

"Hey yourself, cowboy!" she called back, waving as she climbed out.

She slammed her door shut, then leaned against it, crossing her legs at the ankles and shading her eyes to watch him approach.

As always, she looked cool and stylish wearing a crisp blue blouse she'd tucked into her jeans, and vintage boots on her feet. These boots were subdued, compared to her usual preference—golden brown with the distinctive diamond brand of her daddy's ranch, the Dusty Diamond, stamped in a darker shade all over the supple leather.

"You're lookin' good," he said as he drew near.

"Why, thank you," she drawled. Her gaze ran over him in return, from his dusty boots, work-worn jeans and chambray shirt, up to the Stetson he'd pushed back on his head. Shaking her tousled head in disbelief, she glanced past him to the lumber piled by the stables. "And you look like you're working hard."

"I am. Lots to do, and I'm just the man to do it," he agreed, matching her light tone, but he'd almost reached her by then and, this close, could see the strain on her face that belied her nonchalant tone and pose.

Troy stopped in front of her. He casually stripped off his gloves, his gaze sharpening on her face. "So what brings you out here?"

She gave him a smile that didn't quite reach her eyes. "I just wanted to talk to Ally and couldn't get through on her phone," she said lightly. "She around?"

He shook his head. "Sorry, no. She ran into Austin to pick up more cedar posts." Concerned as the distress in her eyes deepened, he added, "She should be back in a couple of hours, if you want to wait."

Misty glanced at the diamond-studded watch on her wrist,

then bit her lip and shook her head. "I'd love to, but I can't." She looked off toward the stables, then drew a deep breath. "It's Daddy. We just got home from the hospital yesterday, but I'm going to take him back. He's…not doing well at all."

"Aw, Mist…" He slapped his gloves against his palm, not knowing what to say. "I'm sorry. Is there anything I can do to help?"

She shook her head again. "There's really nothing anyone can do," she said sadly, then cleared her throat to add, "But can you let Ally know?"

"Sure."

"Thanks." She brushed at her eyes, then took another deep breath and forced a smile. "And you might as well tell her my other news, too. I finally took one of those tests she bought me—and, well, it was positive."

She paused, obviously waiting for his response. But Troy remained silent, simply staring at her. So she put it more bluntly. "I'm pregnant."

He must have looked as stunned as he felt, because Misty studied his face, then added uncertainly, "Ally said she told you she wasn't pregnant, that she bought the tests for me."

Troy drew a deep breath, trying to take it all in, make sense of it all. "She told me she wasn't pregnant," he said carefully. "She never came right out and said the tests were for you, though."

Misty's face cleared. "Oh, well, she was trying to cover for me. She knew I didn't want Cole—or any of her brothers or anyone else—to know I might be pregnant."

Troy felt his jaw tighten. Ally could have told *him*. Okay, so she'd tried to tell him the truth before they were married, and he'd ignored her; she sure hadn't made much of an effort since.

Misty was starting to frown again, so he pushed past Ally's involvement to fasten on another piece of information he wanted clarified. "So Cole's the father."

He knew his voice sounded grim because Misty's expression turned rueful as she patted his arm to soothe him. "Yes, Cole's the father," she confirmed, and then tried to give his arm a shake, adding warningly, "But don't you say a word to him, Troy O'Malley. You promise me, now. This is just between him and me and I plan to tell him myself in my own time. When I'm not so worried about Daddy."

Troy didn't want to promise. What he wanted to do was head on over to the Circle C and break Cole Cabrerra's face.

But the mention of her father had brought Misty's worried look back, and when he didn't reply, her grasp on his forearm tightened. "Please, Troy? As a favor to me?"

"Okay," he agreed grudgingly. "I won't say anything to him until you do." Then he thought grimly, he planned to say plenty. Most likely with his fists.

"He'll probably insist on marrying me."

"He'd better."

"Oh, Troy…"

He glanced at her sharply. "What? I thought you wanted to marry him?"

"Not for that reason. I doubt any woman would." She smiled faintly. "But it would have some benefits. That way, you'll officially be the baby's uncle."

"Official or not, you know I'll always be here for you and the kid."

"Thanks," she said huskily. "It helps to know you're in my corner." Then she added more briskly, "Now, give me a hug. I have to get going."

"I'm sweaty," he warned.

She wrapped her slender arms around him, and gave him a big squeeze. "I don't care. It's not every day I get to tell a man he's going to be an uncle."

Troy hugged her back more carefully, aware of how small and fragile she felt. "An uncle. It's hard to believe." *And not a father like he'd believed.*

As he absorbed the thought, disappointment morphed into anger. At himself for acting like a fool, and at Ally, for stringing him along.

"Yes!" Misty exclaimed, oblivious to his feelings. "And Ally will be an aunt."

Not trusting himself to reply to that, Troy gave Misty one more hug, then pushed her gently away. Holding her by her arms, he met her eyes as he told her, "Now, don't forget to let me know if you need anything. Anything at all."

"I won't," she promised, and broke away to climb back in her car. She started up the motor and rolled down her window. "And don't you forget to tell Ally my news," she instructed him. "And tell her that I want it to remain a secret—just between the three of us—until I get back from Dallas."

"I'll tell her," Troy promised, and stepped back as she drove off.

Oh, yeah, he'd tell her, all right, he thought grimly, eyes narrowed against the dust and bright sun as he watched Misty's car speed down the drive. He planned to tell Ally O'Malley plenty.

Right after he made her pay for letting him think she was pregnant.

Chapter Ten

"It takes two to tangle. When they do, be prepared for posturing and pawing and plenty of bellowing…."
—*Successful Breeding: A Guide for the Cattleman*

Talking to her aunt's lawyer hadn't helped much, Ally decided as she left his office. Not that Alfred Papier hadn't tried to give assistance.

Yes, the little lawyer assured Ally, Eileen Hennessey's will simply stated that in order for Ally to assume control of her inheritance she had to marry. No, a minimum time limit for the marriage hadn't been specified. Well, yes, Cole could contest her assumption of control if the marriage proved fraudulent—that is, entered into merely to circumvent the terms of the will—but no, that didn't mean the court would necessarily rule in his favor. On the other hand, it might.

"Obviously," the little man concluded, "the longer the marriage endures, the stronger your claim."

Which basically confirmed what she'd already known, Ally thought glumly walking slowly toward Troy's truck. That as long as Cole didn't question her marriage to Troy, she was fine. Or—to be more specific—as long as Troy didn't back out of the marriage, making Cole suspicious, she was fine.

But Troy wouldn't do that, she decided. Yes, he might—judging by the monitor and stuffed horses—be a little disappointed when he realized there really was no baby. Okay, he'd probably be angry. But that didn't mean he would back out of their marriage once he learned the truth. He needed that lease.

The best thing to do would be to hurry right home and tell him, Ally thought, her steps slowing even more. Except—she paused, struck by inspiration—except she needed to get her hair trimmed and this would be the perfect time to do it.

With the lease money Troy had given her burning a hole in her bank account, if not her pocket, she bypassed the ten-dollar-a-cut shop she usually favored and went into a more exclusive salon Misty had mentioned. The prices made Ally gasp, but when the stylist finished and she looked into the mirror, her shocked look softened to a smile. Her dark hair was soft and shiny—still long, but layered in a smoother, more sophisticated style that was, she admitted to herself, well worth the price.

Since her hair looked so nice, she decided to have a manicure, choosing Pink Echo polish for her fingernails to show off her ring, as well as a pedicure, selecting Passionate Pink for her toes. When one of the stylists offered to do her eyes and shape her eyebrows, Ally succumbed to that lure, too, and added a new mascara and lipstick to her small store of makeup.

By the time she emerged from the salon, Ally's bank account was a couple of Franklins lighter—so she should have walked right past the white, flirty top she saw in a nearby boutique window without pausing. But the loose, sleeveless, baby-doll style would be cool in the heat, so she went in and bought it, along with strappy sandals, and kept them both on, bagging up her boots and T-shirt.

When she emerged from the boutique the shadows were lengthening. Surprised, Ally hurried to pick up the fencing, but bypassed the grocery store to head for home.

When she got there, she found Troy in the kitchen, washing lettuce at the sink.

"Sorry I'm late. I got held up and—" She broke off, her senses assaulted by the delicious, spicy smell of spaghetti sauce. On the rare occasions she'd come home past dinnertime at the Circle C, she'd usually find her brothers milling around the kitchen, like cattle around an empty feeder, just waiting for someone to toss in hay. They'd never think to go ahead and start supper before she got there.

But Troy had, Ally realized as she looked at the heaping bowl of spaghetti on the table, the sliced bread and the salad he was making, and her tone filled with pleasure. "Oh! You made dinner!"

He turned to look at her. Ally smiled, waiting for him to mention her haircut or her new blouse. His gaze skimmed over her—from her shining dark hair all the way down to her bare toes in her new sandals—but he said simply, "Yeah. Go ahead and sit down. I'm just about done here."

A little disappointed by his lack of response, Ally offered, "I'll help—"

"Sit!"

She sat, startled by his harsh tone.

He returned her surprised look with a bland expression. "Sorry. Didn't mean to bark at you." He gestured toward her toes. "Just thought you'd better get off your feet. They look a little swollen."

"They do?" Dismayed, Ally wiggled her newly painted toes. They looked fine to her—did he really think they looked swollen?

She was still studying them as he joined her at the table. He picked up the noodles and Ally forgot her swollen feet for the moment, watching as he scooped a huge mound of spaghetti, then salad, on her plate, and added a generous helping of sauce and a thick slice of bread. About to protest at the size of the huge serving, Ally bit the words back. He'd cooked, and he obviously wanted her to enjoy his cooking.

She could certainly understand that. With a sigh of appreciation, she started eating a delicious, home-cooked meal that for once, she hadn't had to make herself.

"Oops, forgot the drinks." Troy snagged the wine bottle off the counter that Ally had bought on sale at the Piggly Wiggly to celebrate her inheritance. She'd never gotten around to opening it, but this was as good a time as any to enjoy the sweet Moonstruck Merlot she'd served on special occasions at the Circle C.

Troy untwisted the cap. He tilted the bottle over her glass— then whipped it away again, before even one crimson drop could fall. "Damn! I forgot. You're not supposed to drink wine, are you."

"I'm not? Oh, yeah." Her supposed pregnancy. "I guess not. Although I'm sure one glass wouldn't hurt."

He looked shocked. "Ally O'Malley! Do you want to hurt the baby?"

"Cabrerra," she corrected him. "Of course I don't." If there had been a baby. But there wasn't, and for a minute or two, as she watched him pour himself a generous glass, savor the bouquet, take a healthy swallow—then choke a little—she toyed with the thought of telling him right then and there she wasn't pregnant.

He set down his glass and started eating, and she followed suit, deciding to wait until later to tackle the tricky subject. He'd be mellower after he had eaten, and she didn't want to start a fight during this wonderful meal.

"This is really good," she told him. "Thank you for making it."

He shrugged. "No big deal. It's the one thing I know how to fix." He picked up a slice of bread and ripped off a crusty bite with his strong, white teeth. He chewed, swallowed and added, "I knew you'd be starved. Eating for two and all." He gestured toward her stomach. "That baby is certainly starting to grow, isn't it?"

Ally almost choked on her spaghetti. "Are you saying I'm getting fat?" she asked, when able to speak again.

Troy shook his head. "Not fat at all," he said soothingly. Ally started to relax, only to stiffen again as he added, "Just pregnant."

Ally's cheeks burned with embarrassment. Surely she didn't look like she was pregnant! She took another bite of spaghetti, chewed furiously. Maybe it was the new blouse—it was kind of loose. Maybe it looked like a maternity top. She'd thought it looked fine in the store…but store mirrors could be tricky. Like mirrors in a carnival fun house—the kind that made you look skinnier and taller, only store mirrors weren't so obvious as a carnival mirror, of course.

She'd take the blouse back, she decided, looking down at it. She rubbed at a tiny drop of sauce on the right breast. She'd get this spot out, then find her receipt and demand that—

"Damn, you were hungry, weren't you?"

"Hmm?" Ally glanced blankly at Troy, then down at her plate. And groaned. It was completely empty. She'd been thinking so hard, she'd plowed through her entire meal without realizing it. Good Lord, no wonder she was putting on weight!

She'd cut back at little, she decided as she helped clear away the dishes. She'd never had a weight problem, and she certainly didn't want to develop one now. So she stifled a pang of longing when Troy opened the freezer and pulled out the carton of ice cream she'd sent him out for the night before last. The mint chocolate chip ice cream. Her favorite.

He pried off the lid and glanced inside. "Whoa, this is almost gone."

He glanced at her inquiringly, and Ally admitted, "I had some yesterday afternoon. And a little last night." It had been a very stressful day with all those phone calls.

He lifted his eyebrow. "I see." He set the carton on the counter. Opening the cupboard, he got out a red bowl. "Want some now?" he asked.

Ally resolutely shook her head. "No. I'd better not."

"Oh? Why?"

"My weight."

He chuckled. "You don't need to worry about that."

Her spirits lifted. "I don't?"

He shook his head. "Nah, of course not." He carved out a big scoop of the mint-green ice cream and plopped it in the bowl. "There's nothing wrong with being pudgy—"

Pudgy!

"When you're pregnant. In fact, have you considered the possibility that you might—" another huge scoop landed on the first "—be carrying twins?"

"Twins!" Ally stared at him aghast. "You think I'm carrying twins?"

"With a set in your family, you have to admit it's a possibility."

She refused to admit any such thing. She grabbed the hem of her new top, yanking it up to bare her flat midriff. "Do I *look* like I'm carrying twins?"

Troy froze, the full ice cream scooper poised in midair, his gaze fixed on her stomach. Ally's heart jumped at the smoldering look in his eyes. She sucked in her breath—and her stomach muscles—and felt a corresponding contraction, deep and sharp in her womb.

As if he knew, the heat in Troy's eyes flared—and the ice cream plopped into the bowl.

The small spell broken, Ally hurriedly dropped her blouse.

Troy's lashes lowered, hiding his gaze as he set the scooper down. When he turned back to her, his expression was blandly impersonal, although his voice sounded husky as he said, "Let me see."

Before Ally could stop him, he stepped closer and slid his big hand beneath her shirt. He flattened it on her belly, controlling the involuntarily buck she gave with his other hand, pressed against her lower back. "Easy now," he said, holding her in place. His thumb lightly explored the dimple of her belly button. "Let's see what we've got here."

He spread his fingers and Ally shivered a little at the tickling, teasing sensation of his callused fingertips on her tender skin. Her shirt was raised up, caught on his sinewy forearm, and her jeans rode low on her hips, baring most of her stomach. His tanned hand looked big and brown against her lighter skin, and his long fingers spanned her easily from prominent hip bone to hip bone.

"Hmm," he said thoughtfully, and massaged her tummy gently, causing a blossoming heat between her legs. "Maybe not twins…" He rubbed her again, his fingertips slipping beneath her waistband to nudge the elastic of her bikini panties.

Ally held her breath, closing her eyes as he pressed against her. He bent his head. His breath felt warm against her ear as he asked, "Are there any triplets in your family?"

"Mmm…no— No!" Her eyes shot open. "Of course not!"

Ally pushed his hand away, and stepped back, furiously yanking down her shirt. "I do *not* look like I'm having triplets!"

"Sure you don't." His soothing tone made her grit her teeth.

"But if you do, wouldn't it be a kick to name them Larry, Moe and Curly Joe? After the Three Stooges? I bet the kids would love that." Troy bent down to speak to her belly. "Won't you, guys?"

"Oh, stop!" She pushed him away.

He straightened and regarded her stomach consideringly. "Of course, you *might* be having girls."

"I'm not—"

"You can't be sure of that. But I've got it covered. How 'bout Sally, Hallie and Callie O'Malley?" he asked, drawing the names out with relish. "Kind of has a ring to it, don't you think?"

"I think you're insane."

Striding past him, she went into the front room and plopped on the couch. Okay, he was teasing. He *had* to be teasing. But it didn't matter; she just couldn't take any more talk about their mythical baby. Or babies, as the case might be.

So no more procrastinating. She was going to tell him tonight— as soon as he came in here—that she wasn't really pregnant.

Just really fat.

She frowned and was still frowning when Troy sauntered into the room a few minutes later, the red bowl heaped with mint-green ice cream cradled in his palm.

"You forgot your dessert," he said.

"I don't want any," she said shortly…then changed her mind, as she watched him devour spoonful after spoonful. A little bit wouldn't hurt, she finally decided. It would help cool her down.

She stood up. "Maybe I will have some, after all."

"Sorry. This is the last of it." He held up a spoonful. "Do you want to share?"

"No." She sat again and watched him eat another bite with obvious enjoyment. It looked so good….

Catching her gaze, he smiled at her—a wide, white smile below cunning green eyes. "C'mon, let's share." He moved over—all the way over—to sit right next to her, trapping her in the corner of the couch.

His muscular thigh pressed against hers, making her stomach flutter in excited panic while he rounded up a big spoonful of ice cream from his bowl. "Here you go—"

Ally opened her mouth to refuse—

—and he slipped the spoon in.

Ahh. Ally lowered her lashes, half closing her eyes as the minty, cold creaminess tingled on her tongue. Mmm, it was good. She savored the taste while Troy started talking.

"I forgot to tell you…" He fed her another bite.

This one contained a big chunk of chocolate. Yum!

"While you were gone…" He scooped up another spoonful. Popped it in her mouth. "I drove into Tangleweed…."

"Uh-huh?" The ice cream felt so cool sliding down her throat. Tasted so sweet.

"Stopped in at the library…"

Ally accepted the last bite. It melted in her mouth as she regretfully watched Troy set the bowl aside on the end table. Maybe she could scrape the bottom…

"And I checked out that book you mentioned."

"That's good—what!" Her gaze flashed from the red bowl to his face. "What book?"

"You remember…" He took a moment to stretch, squeezing her farther into her corner, then he rested his arms along the back of the sofa, settling one behind her head. "That Oprah favorite you told me about on our wedding night. *What to Expect When You're Expecting to Expect.*"

"And you *found* it?"

"Janie did, although it took her a while. Seems you were a little off on the title and got the doctor's name wrong again."

"I did?" she asked weakly.

"Yeah. It's not Dr. Spunk, but Stunk."

"Stunk?"

"Uh-huh. And you got your information wrong, too. According to Dr. Stink—"

"Stink?"

"Stunk," he corrected her firmly. "According to Dr. Stunk, sex during the early part of pregnancy can be good for the woman— can help relieve tension. So there's no need to abstain any longer."

He turned. Ally caught a warning flash of vengeful green eyes and then he pounced on her, plastering his mouth over hers.

"Mmmph!" Ally pushed and shoved against the nearly two hundred pounds of solid male crushing her into the cushions. Wriggling and squirming, she finally managed to slip out from beneath him and slid onto the floor.

Her rear landed with a bounce. Immediately Ally scrambled away, but Troy caught her ankle, slowly pulling her back, sliding on her bottom across the floor toward him as he said, "It's not like we haven't done it before—"

"No, we—"

"And we *are* married—"

"But that's—"

"It'll be good for you, Al— Good for *both* of us!"

"No, I—"

"And even good for the baby—"

"There is no baby!" she blurted out, and with an adroit twist of her foot, managed to free her ankle.

Panting, breasts heaving, Ally lay back on her elbows with her knees up and feet flat, ready to scoot again, warily watching Troy, who lay sprawled across the couch, with his arm still stretched out toward her.

His lean, brown hand was mere inches from her ankle. Noting the danger, Ally drew her foot cautiously away.

His eyes narrowed menacingly. "You had me paint this whole damn house."

"You insisted!"

He slowly sat up. "And you said you craved ice cream…."

"I did!" She lifted her chin—took another prudent scoot back. "You don't have to be pregnant to have cravings. Look, it's not my fault that you've been laboring under a major misconception—"

"*Laboring* is right!"

"After all, you're the one," she added hurriedly, "who refused to listen to me when I told you I wasn't pregnant. More than once, in fact."

No, he hadn't listened—because he hadn't wanted to know, Troy realized suddenly. Not because he wanted a baby, although he'd been fine with that when he'd thought one was on the way, but because he'd wanted *her*—Ally. He'd wanted her bound to him by more than a business deal or a piece of paper signed by a judge. He'd foolishly thought the baby was a bond growing between them.

He'd been a fool, all right. A fool not to have been making love to her all along. Well, he wouldn't be making that mistake much longer.

He stood and Ally jumped to her feet, too, demanding, "What are you doing?"

"I'm getting ready to make up for lost time," he said grimly.

"Wait a minute, Troy." Ally faced him across the small room, braced for action. He seemed to shift and Ally tensed a little more, but didn't move. He wouldn't charge her—she knew he wouldn't—if she simply held her ground. The smoldering promise in his eyes made her pulse race, but she met his gaze, saying firmly, "We need to talk."

His jaw set. "There's nothing left to talk about. You're my wife, we're married and we've done it before."

"No, we haven't."

His frown darkened. "Haven't what?"

"We haven't done *it*." She didn't mean to goad him—or maybe she did. Because her voice held an almost accusing note as she added, "You...disqualified yourself the last time by falling asleep before you—we—you know."

Troy's angry, determined expression shifted to stunned amazement, then embarrassment. Ruddy color rose under his tanned cheeks. "The hell you say," he growled.

She nodded. "Yes, I do. So I'm sure you understand why I'm not interested in repeating the experience," she said, almost primly.

That made Troy narrow his eyes again. Prim be damned. "Since we never actually did 'it,' repeating isn't quite the right word." He stepped closer. "Why don't we consider this an all new go-round?"

"Why don't we *not*."

He took another step toward her. "We're married."

"That doesn't matter. We have a business deal, not a marriage. I never intended for sex to be a part of my proposition to gain control of Bride's Price at all."

He gave her a skeptical look. "C'mon, Ally. Give me a break. That wasn't a business suit you were wearing in Big Bob's."

She stiffened indignantly. "Oh! I only wore those clothes to—to—"

"Bait the trap?" he suggested dryly when she paused.

"No! To—to ease the men into talking to me. No one in Tangleweed is interested in talking to Ally Cabrerra, the country girl with four brawling older brothers. Look at how Dan ran off. But before you came over, when Dan thought I was someone else, someone confident and sexy..."

Troy realized his jaw had dropped. He snapped it shut. Was she kidding? She just didn't get it. It wasn't her brothers that kept the cowboys away and it definitely wasn't any lack of sexiness. She didn't need a blond wig to get attention. Hell, she drew male glances everywhere she went. *He* could spot her clear across a rodeo arena in the middle of a crowd.

What kept men at a distance was her unawareness of those glances. Sure, Troy had teased her about old Clancy and Red in Big Bob's, but there'd been plenty of cowboys who would have been thrilled to have caught her eye. And yeah, Dan had taken off when Cole's name came up, but Troy would bet his favorite trophy buckle and all his prize money to boot that if Ally had paid more attention to the clown, Dan wouldn't have left her side.

Instead she'd been distracted by Troy. As much as she'd wanted to ignore him, she hadn't been able to.

He considered that a moment. Maybe, like it or not—and he knew she didn't like it or she wouldn't have invented that ridiculous book to keep him away—Ally was as attracted to him as he was to her.

"Why are you looking at me like that?" she demanded, interrupting his thoughts. Her blue eyes with their thick fringe of dark lashes narrowed suspiciously. "What are you thinking about?"

About you, he thought. *For far too many months I've been thinking about you. Now it's time to do something about it.*

"I'm thinking," he drawled, "about that night in the No-Tell motel. I'm trying to figure out how much I imagined, and how much was real." He drew closer, moving slow and easy. "I remember kissing you…"

Berry pink bloomed in her cheeks.

"…and you kissing me back. And us lying naked in bed together."

Her flush deepened.

Troy stopped in front of her. "I didn't imagine that, did I?"

She bit her lip and averted her gaze.

Troy waited. When she refused to look at him, he reached out to catch her chin, gently tilting it up so he could see her darkened, beautiful eyes. "Kiss me again, Ally," he said huskily, demanding and pleading all at the same time. "Not because we're married or agreed to a business deal. Just because you want to—want me, to finish what we started."

Ally stared up at him. His eyes wouldn't let hers go. She knew she should refuse, step back and move away…but she couldn't.

Instead, she took the last step toward him and wrapped her arms around his neck. His arms immediately circled her waist, holding her close.

"Ally," he said. "Ally…"

He kissed her deeply, thoroughly, as he always did, and he tasted oh so good. Sweeter than the mint, richer than the chocolate she could taste on his tongue. Ally pressed closer as he explored her mouth, logic overcome once again by pure aching need. She shivered when his warm hand slipped beneath her blouse to cover her breast, moaned as his thumb brushed her peaked nipple.

He responded to the small sound by shifting his hold, the arm around her waist tightening as he bent to swing her up into his arms.

Ally held on tight as he strode across the room. She expected him to carry her back to the couch, but he kept going, heading into the pink bedroom. The room was dark, but he strode confidently forward, then stopped, his hold loosening as he laid her down— on the bed, she realized, feeling a mattress beneath her. He must have reassembled the double bed while she was in Austin.

The darkness enveloped her, enhancing her other senses. She inhaled the scents of fresh paint and man. The mattress dipped with Troy's weight as he sat beside her, and her fingers glided across the soft ridges of the quilt beneath her—to find him, to explore the flexing muscles of his broad back as he toed off his boots and yanked off his clothes—while Ally, just like she had before in the No-Tell Motel, lay waiting for him, reaching for him as he turned at last to lie beside her in the darkness. He took her in his arms.

She was a country girl; she knew all the facts. Troy taught her the wonder.

She sighed and gasped with pleasure at the kisses he strung from her breasts to her thighs. Reveled in the hard, warm weight of his body covering hers. She trembled with excitement, with desire, holding him tight as he settled between her legs—pushed inside….

Then he froze. And she knew *he* knew. Not only that he hadn't made love with her, but that she'd never made love with anyone, ever before.

"Ah, Ally," he groaned, and dropped his forehead to rest against hers while he held the rest of his body completely, precariously still. "Something else I didn't know…."

He drew a deep, rasping breath. "Do you want this, babe?" he asked, his voice husky, so thick with need, she could barely understand him. He kissed her mouth, pressed his hips slightly, carefully against hers. "Or…do you want me to stop?"

He waited, poised over her, his chest heaving, his heart pounding against her breasts—beating just as hard, just as fast, Ally realized, as hers.

She slid her hands through his soft, thick hair, curved her fingers around his strong neck to bring his mouth back to hers. *Oh, yes, she wanted this.*

"Don't stop," she whispered against his lips. "Please don't stop."

For a moment, he remained still. Then he moved, carefully but firmly thrusting forward to break through the small barrier keeping them apart. Ally winced at the pain, the price paid by every virgin bride, while her breath caught at feeling him so big and full inside her.

He kissed her, murmured reassurances, and slowly, gradually the pain melted away, replaced by burning pleasure as he thrust again, slowly, steadily…riding her…no, she was riding him, climbing into the darkness…the pleasure inside her growing, tightening until finally—*finally*—it peaked.

And she flew off among the stars.

Chapter Eleven

"Bulls have been known to copulate as frequently as twenty-five times in twenty-four hours…."
—*Successful Breeding: A Guide for the Cattleman*

"Oh, no," Ally moaned, awakening to kisses on her neck the next morning before the chickadees even began to sing. "It's too early," she sighed, turning her face into her pillow and hunching her bare shoulder to escape the warm lips nibbling their way toward hers. "I thought you weren't a morning person. You were always so grumpy before."

"That's because we weren't making love. Making love starts the day out right."

"Sleeping until the sun comes out starts it off even better."

"Not today, sleepyhead," Troy whispered huskily in her ear.

Ally smiled into her pillow, waiting to see what he would do. If he'd kiss her shoulder, her cheek—

She heard a click. Soft light flooded the room.

Blinking at the sudden brightness, Ally grabbed the sheet with a gasp of dismay, yanking it up over her bare breasts. "What are you *doing?*" she asked Troy as he turned away from the lamp he'd switched on to lie back beside her.

He propped himself up on his elbow, one hand supporting his head, the other coming to rest on her stomach. His eyes were heavy lidded, his hair was tousled. Whiskers shaded his square jaw. He idly brushed his thumb back and forth over the small indent of her belly button beneath the thin sheet, as he told her, "We need to talk."

His green eyes studied her face intently, and under his gaze, she felt vulnerable, exposed and definitely a mess. But he was right, they did have things to discuss. So Ally pushed back her hair, meeting his eyes as he began talking.

"Misty came by yesterday while you were out," he said. "She told me to let you know that she's pregnant. With your brother's baby," he added, an acid note creeping into his tone. "But she doesn't want anyone else to know yet."

Ally studied his face but was unable to read his expression. "So what do you think about that?"

"I think Misty's going to do whatever she thinks is best. As to what your brother will do when she eventually tells him…" Troy shrugged. "I have no idea."

Ally didn't, either. Once she would have sworn Cole would definitely want to marry Misty without delay. But once she also would have sworn that her brother loved the pretty blonde and would never break up with her.

Ally sighed. There was just no predicting Cole's behavior. "I went to see Aunt Eileen's lawyer yesterday," she told Troy. "He told me if we decide to end the marriage now—get a divorce— it will be fine as long as Cole doesn't challenge the validity of the marriage."

At the word *divorce,* Troy's hand flattened on her stomach—a warm, solid weight holding her down. His gaze sharpened on her face. "And you don't think he will?"

Ally didn't say anything for a moment, silently admitting to herself she just wasn't sure. "Even if he does," she said finally, "the lawyer says there's a chance that the courts will rule in my favor—let me retain control."

"But there's a chance they won't," Troy said shrewdly.

Reluctantly, Ally nodded. "So what do you think we should do?"

Troy reached out to capture one of her hands. Absently he played with her slender fingers, running his thumb over her wedding ring, while he considered the situation. In order for him to attain control of the Running M, he still needed the deed to Bride's Price. Mick had done his part by signing over the controlling interest; Troy still needed to do his.

If Cole regained control of Bride's Price, however, Troy knew the other man would never sell to Troy. But give it a couple more weeks—maybe a month, 'cause she could be so darn stubborn—and he should be able to persuade Ally into seeing reason. Especially now that they were lovers.

He could spare a month to be with Ally. Besides, it might be smart to wait before taking on the management of the Running M, anyway. With the rodeo circuit heating up, he'd have more time to concentrate on working out and getting ready to compete while staying at Bride's Price than he would overseeing and implementing the changes he planned at the much bigger property.

Yeah, staying here, getting the place in top condition—because he still had a few things he wanted to do yet—while convincing Ally to invest in another property for her horse breeding, or better yet come stay at the Running M with him—made a lot of sense.

"I think we should wait before getting a divorce. Leave things as they are for the next month or so. Give Cole more time to adjust," he added, although personally he suspected they could be married for a hundred years and the other man would never give in.

But Ally nodded, obviously relieved by his decision.

Troy ran his thumb over her ring again, then lifted up her hand to look at it. "Pretty."

"It is a beautiful ring," Ally admitted.

"I meant your hand," he said, brushing a kiss across her knuckles. With her hand to his mouth, he slanted her a considering glance and drawled, "There's just one more thing to discuss…."

Ally tilted her head inquiringly. "What's that?"

"I forgot to use protection," he said against her fingers. "Again."

"Omigod!" Ally sat bolt upright, forgetting her sheet and jerking her hand out of his hold.

"Not that it mattered before, since I—how did you put it?—disqualified myself." A small smile played around his mouth, then disappeared. His eyes darkened as he stared at her breasts, and he reached out to touch her nipple. "But it might this time."

Seeing where his hand was headed, Ally yanked her sheet up, clutching it over her breasts as she mentally reviewed her personal calendar.

"I'm sure we'll be okay," she said at last in relief. "But we can't do this again."

"I know. I promise I'll use a rubber from now on."

"I mean, we shouldn't be doing *this*—" she waved her hand to indicate the rumpled bed, them in it "—at all. It…complicates things."

Troy stared at her—taking in her frowning blue eyes, her pink cheeks and swollen mouth. Her bare shoulders and the silky, sexy tangle of her dark hair.

She *had* to be kidding.

Reaching out, he tumbled her against his chest as he settled against his pillows. He gave her a reproving look. "C'mon, Ally, that's crazy talk. You know you can't keep your hands off me," he said, keeping his arms clamped firmly around her as she tried to sit up again.

"I can't?" she said dryly, abandoning her struggle to look up at him with her head on his shoulder.

"No," he said firmly. "Or your eyes, either." He tapped her nose admonishingly. "I saw you watching me at the Houston rodeo last spring."

She wrinkled her nose and pushed away his hand. "Oh, I watched you, all right—the way I watch that bad-tempered hound that Willie Pitts owns. I keep an eye on it so I can stay out of its way and don't get bitten."

He lifted her hand to his mouth and nibbled on the tips of her slender fingers. "I'm not the one who bites...."

She snatched her hand from his grasp and tugged on his chest hair.

"Ouch!" He grabbed her fingers again in self-defense. "Talk about bad-tempered—okay, okay—" He squeezed her tight as she tried to get free again. "All I want here is the truth. Because I'm pretty sure I noticed you noticing me plenty in Houston."

He could feel her lips curl into a smile against his chest, and she said primly, "I wasn't noticing you so much as the women making fools of themselves over you."

She absently ran her small callused finger up over his chest and across his flat nipples, unknowingly making Troy harden as she added, "All my life you've just been part of the landscape— that arrogant Troy O'Malley who'd get my brothers all riled up. Even when I came up with my proposition to get Bride's Price, I never, ever thought of asking you for help."

No, Troy remembered, his good mood fading a bit. She'd thought of asking Theodore-be-damned-Bayor.

But after he'd seen her in Big Bob's bar, dressed for man hunting, and learned about her "proposition"—hell, Troy thought, there'd been no way he would have let her out the door with any other male.

Just considering the possibility caused a wave of possessiveness to rise up in his chest. He shifted, rolled on top of her, completely covering her soft, slender body with his much bigger, much harder one. He rose up on his elbows and slid his hands through her tousled hair, cradling her head as he looked into her face.

Mine, he thought, meeting her eyes, dark and startled in the soft morning light. *Only mine.*

"We're married," he said huskily, "and we might as well enjoy it. So give me a kiss, Ally O'Malley."

"Cabrer—"

Before she could finish, he covered her mouth with his.

Troy, Ally discovered in the next three weeks, was insatiable. He made her insatiable, too.

They made love everywhere—on the couch in the living room, and on the back screened-in porch. Precariously, in the wide rope hammock in the middle of a hot afternoon. Anywhere Troy could persuade Ally to try.

But because he was truly an old-fashioned guy at heart, Troy's favorite place to make love with Ally was in the big bed in the pink bedroom until late into the warm summer nights, then again in the early cool dawn as the sun crept in through the uncovered window to bathe the room in a soft, rosy glow.

If Ally had half expected that finding out she wasn't pregnant would dampen Troy's enthusiasm for working on Bride's Price, during the following weeks she discovered she was wrong. Troy was more energetic than ever. He not only finished repairing the fence and installed his herd in the northeast pasture, he also started fencing another section of grazing land with plans to lease that also in the future as his herd expanded. He worked out longer in the big barn on the gym equipment. He even helped Ally spray-paint the barn and stables.

With cattle to work, Troy brought cutting horses over from the Running M and every day they rode out together, checking on the stock and fences, or simply exploring the sweet little property with its beautiful old trees, creeks and small lake, fed by the foaming Veil falls. Oh, how Ally had missed riding every day. She missed Old Boomer, too, and decided to bring him to Bride's Price. Her brothers were too busy, she knew, to give the sorrel the carrots and special attention he'd grown used to from Ally, and although he was too worn to work cattle anymore, she knew Boomer would enjoy going for gentle rides in the cool of the evening.

So Ally called the Circle C to tell her brothers she'd be coming to get the horse. To her surprise, Luke offered to trailer him over for her the next day and save her the trouble—an offer she was happy to accept.

When she told Troy over dinner about Luke's impending visit, he replied, "I won't be around tomorrow afternoon. I have some business to attend to."

His voice held a curt, clipped note—the same note it had held when he'd told her that Misty was pregnant. Noting his frown, Ally decided not to ask what his business might be. She knew Troy was angry at Cole, and she suspected he simply didn't want to see Luke, either. If that was the case, she didn't want to know.

So Troy wasn't there when Luke arrived the next afternoon in the blue truck, pulling the horse trailer. Ally smiled at the sight of Old Boomer's withers, visible in the trailer's back window, and hurried over to greet the newcomers.

"Hey, little sis." Luke's white grin widened as he climbed out of the cab, and he gave her a hug. "How's it going?"

"Fine." Ally hugged him back, then frowned into his blue eyes, shaded by his brown Stetson. "How are you? You seem thinner."

"Hell, I am thinner," he said ruefully, squeezing her again, then setting her aside to stride to the back of the trailer. "We're all thinner," he told her as he lowered the creaky gate. "Kyle's been doing the cooking."

"Oh, no."

"*Oh, no,* is right. I think he's trying to kill us. Last night he wasn't happy with the chili he'd made so he threw in some bananas. Called it Tropical Tex Mex. Yeah—" Luke grimaced in agreement with the face Ally made "—it was bad. The saddest part is, we all ate it."

"I'll give you some simple recipes," Ally promised, watching as he carefully backed the old horse down the ramp. "Ones that even Kyle can't mess up."

Luke flashed another white smile. "Sounds like a plan," he drawled, leading Boomer away from the truck as the big chestnut reached the bottom.

Ally took the lead from him and Luke slammed the trailer gate closed again. Then he paused, pushing his Stetson back on his forehead to scan the small, neat property with its freshly painted house, big red barn and newly rebuilt corral and stables.

Luke gave a low whistle. "Place is lookin' good, Al. You've done a lot here."

"Troy did most of it," Ally told her brother.

Luke dismissed her comment with a shrug of his wide shoulders, but his smile faded, as he slanted a glance at her. "So, how's it going with him?"

Ally frowned, not liking his tone. "It's going fine," she said emphatically.

Luke's bright blue eyes narrowed on her face. "I wondered if he might be here when I arrived, but I saw him heading north on the Diamond Mine road."

The road that led to the Dusty Diamond. Misty's home.

"So?" Ally said. "What are you trying to say?"

Luke studied her for a second, his usual grin nowhere in sight. "What I'm saying is, Troy O'Malley's already caused trouble between Cole and Misty. I just don't want him to hurt you, too."

"After talking to Misty, it seems to me that Cole's responsible for his own trouble."

Luke considered that a moment, then shrugged again. "Maybe some. But Mick O'Malley has it out for our family. Did you know he tried to buy up the mortgage on the Circle C after Dad died?"

Ally's eyes widened. "No."

"Yeah. Luckily, Cole managed to scrape the money together to pay it off, but it wasn't easy. And if Mick was in on that, you can bet Troy probably was, too."

Ally shook her head, her eyes meeting her brother's without wavering. "That's not true, Luke," she said quietly. "Troy isn't at all like his grandfather."

Luke's lips compressed into a thin line. "Yeah, he is, Al. *That* cowboy can't be trusted."

Ally stiffened. "That cowboy is my husband. And he's been nothing but kind to me." She took a deep breath. "I'm not pregnant, Luke. I never was. But when he thought otherwise Troy stepped up to claim the baby without hesitating. He didn't have to do all this—" her hand swept out to indicate the house, the barn and stables "—he did it to help me out."

She wished she could tell Luke how Troy had invested in businesses in Tangleweed, too, because her brother didn't look convinced.

"Just be sure he's not helping himself out in some way," he warned her.

Ally put her hands on her hips. "Now, how would he be doing that?"

"I'm not sure except—you're a beautiful woman, Al—yeah, you are," he admitted. His rueful grin reappeared in response to the skeptical look she gave him, but his eyes stayed serious as he added, "And Troy O'Malley is drawn to beautiful women— even if you are a Cabrerra."

"O'Malley."

"Huh?" Luke cocked his dark head.

"I'm an O'Malley now, not a Cabrerra," she said. Surprised at her own admission, she added firmly, "I'm Ally O'Malley."

"Crap." Luke stared at her blankly. "That's sadder than Kyle's banana chili."

"Oh, get out of here." Ally gave his hard shoulder a small shove. "I swear, if you say one more thing, I'm not going to give you the chocolate chip cookies I made for you to take back."

Cowed by the threat, Luke shut up. Fifteen minutes later he took off for home, a cookie stuffed in his mouth, a couple more in the hand he used to wave goodbye with out the window.

Ally waved back until the blue truck with the empty trailer rattled out of sight, smiling as she wondered if any of the cookies would make it back to the Circle C. But her smile faded as she collected Old Boomer, patiently waiting by the fence, to lead him down the path to the stables.

So even Luke thought that there was—or rather had been— something between Misty and Troy, she mused. Well, she still didn't believe Misty liked Troy as anything more than a friend.

But how did Troy feel about Misty? a small voice argued inside her head. *Just because Misty doesn't love Troy, doesn't mean he doesn't love her.*

Oh, just stop it, she ordered herself. Even if Troy had gone to the Dusty Diamond today, that didn't mean anything. There were a thousand and one reasons for him to go there, including the one she thought the most likely: so he could avoid seeing one of her brothers.

That thought didn't make her feel much better. Not wanting to think about it anymore, she headed into the stables to break up bales to spread in the stalls, and get Old Boomer settled.

She'd finished spreading straw in the first stall and had installed Boomer there for company while she worked on the one next to him when Troy's voice interrupted her work. "So here you are."

Ally paused. Resting her pitchfork on the floor, she turned to find Troy checking out Old Boomer, who'd hung his big bony head over the stall door to check out the newcomer in return.

"Hey there, old fella." Troy waited patiently while Boomer took huffing breaths of his gray hat and shirt, then reached up to gently rub the sorrel's white muzzle. "I see Luke made it over with your horse."

"Yes," Ally said, as Troy gave Boomer a last pat before sauntering over to rest his arms on the door where she was working. "He left a couple of hours ago."

From the grunt he gave in response, Ally deduced Troy wasn't interested in talking about her brother's visit. Instead, he moved on to one of his preferred topics—himself. "Did you miss me?" he asked.

Actually, Ally had. But he looked so sexy with his green eyes gleaming at her beneath heavy lids, and the tiniest of smug smiles on his mouth, that she certainly wasn't going to tell him so.

"I was busy." She glanced pointedly around the stall. "I was working."

Troy's gaze swept the stall, too, then returned to meet hers. "So I see," he agreed solemnly, but with his eyes crinkling at the corners.

"And now—" she leaned her pitchfork against the wall "—I need to get into the kitchen and make dinner. So, if you'll just step aside…" She made a shooing gesture, as if he was an overly large, pesky fly.

Troy didn't move.

Ally stepped toward him.

He straightened. But instead of stepping away from the half door so she could open it, his green gaze cut to the pile of straw she'd raked together, before returning to travel leisurely from her hair—damp and curly from perspiration where it had escaped from her ponytail, down over her dusty John Deere T-shirt and faded jeans, to the scuffed brown boots Linc had outgrown at ten, before moving back up to meet her eyes once again.

Ally recognized that look. She frowned.

He smiled.

Her frown deepened. "No," she said firmly.

Troy lifted a dark brow. "No what?"

"No, to what you're thinking."

Troy lifted both eyebrows in contrived surprise. "You think you can read my mind?"

"It isn't difficult," Ally said dryly. "Ninety percent of the time, you're only thinking about one thing."

"What's that?"

"Sex."

His green eyes flared.

Her blue eyes narrowed. "You're thinking you'd like to make love on that pile of straw."

"Ally, Ally, Ally…" He shook his head reprovingly. "You're obviously the one obsessed with sex. I wasn't thinking that at all—until you put the idea in my mind. But now that you have…" He lifted the latch and—before she could dart past—slid into the stall and closed the door behind him. Then he blocked it, standing with his booted feet braced and his hands on his hips. "I guess I'll take you up on your suggestion."

"Troy…" Ally said warningly, trying not to smile.

But in the end, Ally didn't need much persuasion at all to give in. Troy just kissed her and kissed her, everywhere he could until finally it was Ally who pulled him down on the pile of straw, Ally who tossed aside his hat and unbuttoned his shirt and his jeans while he undid her clothes.

Ally didn't notice the scratchy straw while they made love. All she could think about was Troy, and the way he made her feel. It wasn't until she drifted back to awareness that Ally became aware of the pieces poking in some very uncomfortable places.

In the stall next door, Old Boomer snorted his disgust. "Boomer disapproves," she told Troy, who lay sprawled heavily on top of her.

"What else can you expect from a gelding?" Troy muttered without lifting his head from where it lay on her breasts. He sighed and his breath flowed over her heated skin in a cooling puff. "Damn, this is comfortable."

He might be comfortable; she wasn't. He weighed a ton and she was *hot.* "Troy…" She pushed at his shoulder. "You're heavy."

He snorted, sounding remarkably like Boomer. "That's your fault. You're the one feeding me all the time."

"Move!"

He groaned in protest but shifted to lie beside her.

That was better, Ally decided, laying her head on his shoulder after she'd pulled up her pants and adjusted her shirt to protect her skin from the straw. Now she was comfortable. Maybe she'd take a short nap…. Her eyes drifted shut….

"Ally…" Troy kissed her cheek. Her eyelids.

She kept them closed. "No. No more." She meant it this time. "I'm resting."

"There you go, giving me ideas again. Actually, in all this excitement—" he teasingly nuzzled his rough chin against her neck, tickling her and making her squirm "—I forgot to tell you the big news. Open your eyes."

Reluctantly, Ally lifted her lashes to find Troy propped up on an elbow leaning over her, his green eyes drowsy with satisfaction as he met her gaze. He looked rumpled and tough and irresistible, Ally thought.

She reached up to brush a piece of straw from his tousled brown hair, and he turned his head, pressing a warm kiss into her palm. The piercing sweetness of the gesture made her throat constrict, and her voice sounded husky as she prompted, "Big news? What's that?"

"I bought you a couple of horses. Two mares." He kissed her palm again, holding her hand pressed against his mouth. Ally could feel his smile as he added, "Peruvian Pasos."

Her breath caught. Her heart seemed to jump, then expand with excitement. A warm flush of joy washed over her. To give her a gift like that he *had* to love her....

"Are you kidding?" she breathed.

Troy shook his head. "Nope. I'm as serious as a pimple on prom night. I struck the deal this afternoon, and you should have the mares before the end of the week. Now all you need to get started is a foundation stallion." He kissed her hand again and rubbed his thumb over her ring. "I gave Stan your number. He'll be calling to make arrangements to bring the mares over."

"Stan?"

Troy nodded. "Yeah. Stan Gunderland. Misty's selling off stock, trying to raise some quick cash. I picked up the mares, and I'm buying her other horses and some of her cattle, as well."

Ally stared up at him, the warm glow fading as his words sunk in. He hadn't bought the horses to help her achieve her dreams, but to help Misty. Which meant love wasn't involved at all. At least, not love for Ally.

The realization left her feeling flat and slightly forlorn. Which was stupid of her. Buying Misty's stock to help her out financially was the same kind of thing Troy had done when he'd invested in Big Bob's Bar and the Jeromes' No-Tell Motel, and who knew how many other business in Tangleweed. She admired that about him; she was glad he was helping Misty. What made her feel sad and even a bit weepy was the fear that this time, Troy wasn't just being kind and neighborly. That he loved her brother's ex-fiancée.

It wasn't something she could easily ask him. Even if she could find the right words, the moment was lost.

Troy had surged to his feet and was slapping his pants and ruffling his hair to get the chaff out. He removed a couple of straws sticking in his shirt. "Not the most comfortable place to make love—" he gave her a wink "—but I'm not complaining."

"Because you weren't on the bottom." Ally sat up slowly, becoming painfully aware of various small aches she hadn't noticed while making love. She felt bruised and dusty and tired—so very tired. Even her arms seemed heavy as she raised them to comb her fingers through her hair, trying to get out some of the straw.

The way she felt must have shown somehow, because Troy's brows slanted in a frown, and he squatted in front of her.

"Hey," he said softly. Catching her chin, he gently tilted her face up to study her eyes. "You okay, sweetheart?"

For no good reason, Ally wanted to cry. The concern in his deep voice, the easy endearment, made her eyes burn. Which was stupid—*she* was being stupid.

The worry on his face deepened. "I thought you'd be happy about the mares."

"I am happy," she said huskily, pulling away from his touch.

"It's a wonderful surprise. I'm just itchy," she said, wiping at her eyes. "The dust makes my eyes water. And I'm getting hungry."

His frown cleared. He rose to his feet. "Me, too." Grinning at her muttered "Now there's a huge surprise," he held out his hand. "C'mon, lazybones. Get up and let's go eat."

"Lazybones!"

She put her hand in his and he pulled her to her feet with easy strength, then held on to her hand all the way back to the house and into the kitchen. Once there, she put him to work. Troy, she'd discovered during the five weeks they'd lived together, liked to cook—or at least, he liked to help her cook, she amended mentally. So she set him to making salad, while she threw together an easy dinner of steak and twice-baked potatoes, and popped a shortcake in the oven to have with strawberries for dessert.

They set the table together, then sat to eat. Troy had second helpings of everything, eating as if he hadn't consumed a huge breakfast and a substantial lunch only hours before, while discussing the deal he'd made with Stan Gunderland in enthusiastic detail.

Ally listened and tried to appear thrilled—and she was, she told herself. She loved the mares Troy had bought. But she couldn't accept them as a gift; it wasn't as if he was really her husband. They'd have to set up some kind of payment plan or something. They needed to discuss the issue, but he looked so pleased with himself that she just couldn't start the argument she knew her decision would cause.

She'd do that tomorrow. She just wasn't feeling well tonight. Maybe it was the barbecue sauce, she thought, watching Troy shaking the bottle over his steak. He'd picked up the brown bottle in town, and brought it home, assuring Ally she was going to love it. She didn't. Not only did the spicy smell turn her stomach, the sauce was so thick, Troy finally had to use a knife to coax it from the bottle.

She pushed her plate away and bypassed the strawberry short-cake that Troy practically inhaled. Instead, she had a cup of tea and a small scoop of mint chocolate ice cream to soothe her unsettled stomach.

By the time they'd both finished, Ally was glad to clear away the plates. The strange lassitude still plagued her, and the lingering smell of the barbecue sauce almost made her gag. She just wanted to go lie down and stop thinking about Troy and Misty, stop wondering if he was in love with the pretty blonde. She tried to put the subject from her mind as she washed the dishes and he dried them beside her, but it wasn't until they were almost done that she finally succeeded.

All it took was Troy saying casually, "I'd better gather my gear tonight if I want to get an early start for the rodeo tomorrow."

Ally whirled to face him, the washcloth clutched in her hand. "You're going to the rodeo tomorrow? The one in Houston?"

He'd sat at the table, the dish towel draped over his broad shoulder, his long legs sprawled as he leaned back in the chair. His hair was still mussed from their lovemaking, but the happy, satisfied look he'd worn since then faded as he stared at her.

He lifted a brow. "Of course I'm going. It's part of the circuit."

"But your knee—"

"It's fine."

It had to be, Ally realized. It hadn't held him back from working out for hours at a time or around the ranch and, now that she thought about it, she hadn't seen him limp for weeks. Still…

"Why don't you skip it this time around?" she asked.

"Skip it?" He stared at her as if she'd suggested he go out and rob the Piggly Wiggly. "I'm not going to skip it. I'm going to *win* it."

He paused, waiting for her to say something. When she remained silent, he asked, "Don't you want to go?"

"No."

He was starting to frown. "I thought you liked rodeos."

"I do." She did like rodeos. Rodeos were good for towns like Tangleweed, bringing in money for the businesses and vendors, as well as providing a way for often-poor ranching kids, like Kyle, to win prize money and even scholarships.

She loved the crowds, the excitement—seeing everyone all duded up in fancy Western shirts, beautiful boots and flashing silver jewelry. She loved watching all the events—seeing the cowboys compete. She even enjoyed the bull riding, most of the time.

But when someone she cared about was on the back of the nearly two-ton beasts, she hated the sport—became literally sick with fear. She'd lost too many people in her life to be able to watch someone she loved taking dangerous risks. She couldn't stand watching Kyle ride, and now, she discovered, she couldn't bear the thought of Troy riding, either.

She clutched the sink, fighting the urge to throw up. "I like rodeos," she said slowly, "but I'm not really in the mood to go. I thought I'd make fried chicken for dinner tomorrow." She looked at him pleadingly. "Can't you miss just this one?"

"It's on the circuit," he said curtly, scowling now. "I've already missed nearly two months."

"But—"

"I'm not going to skip it. I can't. If I do, I can just forget about the Nationals altogether this year."

Ally wanted to continue arguing—to plead with him not to compete. He could get hurt. Forget about his knee, he could break his neck.

But he wore an expression she recognized all too well. An expression her brothers wore every time she tried to convince them not to smoke or drink too much; not to race their trucks on twisting back roads or participate in dangerous extreme sports.

It was the stubborn, implacable expression every man wore when he was determined to do something stupid. Something that might get him hurt. Or even get him killed.

And nothing anyone could say would stop him.

At least, not anything Ally could say. Troy had refused to listen when she'd first told him she wasn't pregnant. He was refusing to listen to her now.

So she turned away to face the sink, saying over her shoulder, "Fine, then. Go. Have fun. I hope you win."

"Aren't you coming with me?" he demanded. "I thought you could watch me ride."

"No!"

If Troy was startled by her outburst, Ally was horrified. She found she was gripping the edge of the sink so hard that her fingers hurt. Carefully she released it, and with a trembling hand reached into the soapy water to pull the plug.

Without looking at him, she said, "Nope. Sorry. I have better things to do with my time."

Without saying another word, she walked out of the kitchen.

Better things to do.

Every time Troy thought about the words, remembered how dismissive Ally had sounded, how distant and aloof she'd acted, he became so enraged he wanted to kick something.

But he restrained himself—except for a bucket that had been left in the stables instead of near the pump where it belonged—because if she could be cool and disdainful, then, damn it! so could he.

If she had better things to do than come watch him ride, watch him take first place—win a silver buckle and bring home the purse—he had better things to do than worry about her. Damned if he'd hang around—obviously just free labor as far as she was concerned—and miss the chance to raise his rankings for the Nationals, which, as she'd so scornfully pointed out that night at Big Bob's, had gone down several slots this past year.

So he coolly climbed into his truck before dawn the next morning without even saying goodbye—which he would have done, because unlike *some* people, he wasn't one to hold a grudge—except Ally had chosen to sleep in the attic room the previous night, and hadn't come down even when he'd rattled the pans loud enough to wake a groundhog in winter as he made himself breakfast. Not that he cared if she couldn't bother to say goodbye. Or wanted to sleep alone. Sleeping alone didn't bother him one bit. The only reason he'd been restless was because every time he dozed off, he'd reach for her—which woke him up and made him angry all over again when he'd remember why she wasn't there.

So, if he was tired, bleary-eyed and still plenty angry as he pulled into the rodeo grounds two hours later, that was her fault. Not that anyone seemed to notice. He greeted friends, checked out the rough stock and his draw for the first go-round, and had deep discussions with his fellow PBR members about everyone's prospects for the fall Nationals.

He did what he always did. What he'd done hundreds of times before at hundreds of rodeos just like this one before he competed— he walked around to enjoy the atmosphere, to absorb the excitement of the people around him, to spike up even higher the adrenaline that always zipped through his veins before a big ride.

But everything felt strange, just a little bit off. Not quite as fun as it should have been. The sun was too hot, the whole place was too crowded. The bright colors of the rodeo banners and promotion signs seemed dim. The usual mouthwatering scents of fajitas, fried chicken and barbecued ribs didn't smell as enticing, and not even his longtime *help-you-to-a-heart-attack* favorites of sausage kebobs and deep-fried Oreos eased the empty feeling in his gut.

The cowboy bunnies were cute enough, he supposed, but the only female that drew his attention was a bald, six-month-old charmer with big blue eyes who, when chucked under her drooly chin, gave a great big smile displaying two tiny front teeth. A future biter, for damn sure.

Yeah, he went through the motions as the day dragged on, but he couldn't stop thinking about Ally. He'd wanted her to come watch him ride. She knew he did, yet she'd refused.

Maybe she thought upsetting him would help her brother Kyle win the pot.

Well, good luck with that, Troy thought, clenching his jaw, because nothing was going to keep him from winning. And, since he knew from more than a decade of competing that anger wasn't going to help him stay on the back of a bull, he needed to get his mind on business.

The timed events had ended, and the arena dragged and watered in preparation for the rough-stock events, so he strolled over to a deserted spot at the rails to rest his arms along a higher board and prop his boot on a lower.

Staring at the tip of his sharkskin boot, he worked at visualizing the upcoming ride from start to finish. Mentally, he put on his protective vest, tightened his chaps, pulled on his glove and picked up the rosin, which would aid his grip on his bull rope when he climbed down onto the broad back of—hell, what was his draw?—spotted, with a twisted horn… Oh, yeah. Twisted Mister.

Gritting his teeth, he started over again, concentrating harder, rebuilding a mental picture of the ride ahead, his surroundings dimming as he imagined settling on Twisted Mister, feeling the raging power of the beast beneath him—

Damn! Troy swore silently as the soft jangle of spurs coming up behind him broke his concentration once again. The fence shook as a booted foot landed next to his on the rail. A huge brown boot, worn and scuffed, with the dust in the ankle creases half hidden by a drag of leather chap fringe.

With a long-suffering sigh, Troy turned his head to see who'd joined him.

Two of Ally's brothers, Kyle—the owner of the boot—and one of the twins, leaned on the railing next to him. The twin wasn't smiling, which, Troy figured, meant he had to be Linc. A lifetime's unsought acquaintance with the Cabrerra look-alikes had taught Troy how to tell them apart. Basically, Luke smiled most of the time, except when he was fighting, while Linc rarely smiled, except when he fought.

"Isn't this a treat," Troy said sourly, and looked out over the arena.

"Howdy to you, too, O'Malley," Kyle drawled.

The twin didn't say anything. So yeah, it had to be Linc.

"So, O'Malley, you ready to lose?" Kyle asked, flashing him a wide white smile.

You ready to get your teeth bashed in? Troy wondered, but ignored the other man. He wasn't in the mood for the usual trash talk with Ally's brothers.

"'Cause I'm gonna take the whole damn thing," Kyle said tauntingly. "Both go-rounds. Make my little sister proud."

Not if he could help it, Troy thought grimly. Besides… "Even if you do win—which, hell, we both know isn't going to happen—your little sister won't be here to see it. Ally stayed at the ranch."

The admission triggered a wave of frustration so intense, Troy's jaw tightened to an ache. The emotion felt familiar, he realized. It was the same frustration he used to feel when Ally so assiduously ignored him.

But this was worse, a hundred times worse, because they were married now. She was his wife. He'd thought she *cared* about him.

He dropped his foot to the ground and moved from the rails, angry at her goading brothers, angry at Ally, but mostly angry at himself for letting the Cabrerras get to him. This was no way to get his head straight.

He turned away, determined to find a quieter, less crowded, Cabrerra-free place to concentrate. He had no trouble ignoring Kyle's taunting, "She'll be missing a good show" as he started walking, but paused when Linc spoke up.

"Ally never watches Kyle ride," the younger man drawled.

Troy turned around, hands on hips, narrowing his gaze on Linc's lean, sardonic face. "What are you talking about? I've seen her watching the bull riding hundreds of times."

"She wasn't watching *Kyle*," Linc told him. "Ally can't stand seeing someone she cares about in danger of getting hurt." His rare, slow smile dawned. "No matter how much she might think the stubborn jackass deserves it."

Troy stared at him, feeling as if he'd been kicked in the chest. Or maybe the head. Thinking hard, he looked out over the arena, watching unseeingly as a bronc rider got tossed and Wilson rushed in, flapping his purple cowboy hat in front of the loose roan to distract it from the fallen rider.

Something had changed, he realized. *He'd* changed. To succeed at the extreme sport, a bull rider had to put everything else but the beast beneath him from his mind. The crowd, the prize, fear—all of it forgotten. He needed to stay in the moment, focused only on the eternal eight-second ride. So when, Troy wondered, had his focus changed?

When had he started riding for Ally?

Because that's what he'd been doing for almost a year now. Hell, no wonder his average had gone down. At every rodeo he'd watch for her—elated when he saw her, disappointed if he didn't. She'd been the one he'd wanted to impress, that he thought of every time he climbed down on a bull. The clear mind he'd needed had been filled with Ally.

His heart started to pound as another thought occurred. She'd changed, too. Ally used to watch him ride, with no apparent problem. But she'd looked almost angry last night when he'd told her he'd be competing today….

So maybe, if Linc was right, Troy thought, maybe her refusal to come today meant she cared about him.

He reached in his pocket for his phone to call her—then realized he'd left it at home. Didn't matter; he needed to see her in person, anyway. After this go-round he'd— No, he didn't want to ride. He wanted to see Ally as quickly as possible. If he rode, he might hurt his knee again, or break something and be laid up like he'd been the last time, unable to make love to her for weeks or even months. No silver or gold buckle or any amount of prize money was worth that.

Besides, how stupid would it be to ride for a woman who hated it when he climbed on a bull?

"See ya, Linc. Good luck, Kyle." Troy slapped him on the back. "I'm outta here."

Linc just nodded, but Kyle looked as stunned as if Troy had slapped him across the face. His dark brows jerked together over his narrowed blue eyes. "What d'ya mean by that, O'Malley?"

"I mean I'm withdrawing and I hope you win."

He started walking away, not even pausing when Kyle bellowed after him, "What? Are you giving up? Afraid of a challenge?"

"Nope," Troy retorted, without looking back. "I just have a bigger challenge waiting at home."

Chapter Twelve

"Unfortunately, not all breeding programs produce the desired results...."

—Successful Breeding: A Guide for the Cattleman

The day felt never-ending to Ally. She was tired. She hadn't been able to sleep at all in the small bed in the attic. She'd still been lying awake when she'd heard Troy in the kitchen, rattling pans as he fixed himself something to eat. He finally stopped, but she waited until she heard his truck pull away before she crept downstairs and into the pink bedroom.

He'd made the bed. She pulled back the covers, anyway, and climbed in, curling up on *his* side, laying her head in the slight depression he'd left on his pillow. The sheets had cooled, his warmth was gone. But beneath the fragrance of fabric softener on the pillowcase, she caught his faint, familiar scent. Soothed, she dozed for a couple of hours, then, still feeling groggy, forced herself to get up and dressed.

Anger had disappeared, but worry lingered, a painful fist in her stomach. She couldn't eat, but she watered and fed the horses. She curried Boomer, making his graying coat shine, stroking slowly through his mane while trying not to think about whether Troy—or Kyle—had competed yet. Whether they'd been hurt.

The heat outside grew unbearable, so she went indoors and tried to stay busy—doing the laundry, washing the floors, making a casserole. But by afternoon she headed outdoors again, desperate for a more taxing job to provide a physical release for the tension tightening inside her.

She walked down to the stables. The shadowy interior felt cool compared to the scorching heat outside, but the sweet, heavy scent of fresh bales filled the air, evoking memories of the day before. Ally retrieved her pitchfork, averting her gaze from the pile of straw where they'd make love, and walked to the other side of the breezeway.

She got down to work, breaking the bales, shaking loose the pieces, ignoring the ache in her arms and in her back, the sweat drenching her body, moving constantly. But in the midst of her almost frenetic activity a part of her was still. Waiting. Listening for Troy's truck. Yearning for his return so she could shed her fear and feel happy again.

And suddenly Ally knew, as if her aunt stood there in the shadows beside her whispering in her ear, why Eileen Hennessey had never returned Bride's Price to Mick O'Malley. Because she'd wanted *him* to hunger and yearn—if not for her, then at least for the land he'd supposedly given with his heart. Eileen had spent her life quietly going through the motions of living, cloaked in sadness, hoping he'd love her again.

But it had never happened, Ally thought, pitching straw automatically, hardly noticing the fine bits that drifted into her hair and clung to her damp skin. Because the Mick O'Malley who'd courted and won a sweet, shy Irish girl no longer existed—had ceased to exist the day he'd sold his love and the life he'd promised to Eileen for money and the Running M. Leaving Eileen waiting, always waiting for his return to—

"Miz O'Malley?"

Ally gasped, dropping the pitchfork and whirling to face the dark figure silhouetted in the sunlit doorway.

A cowboy stood there. Not Mick finally coming to make amends, as she'd thought for one startled moment, but Stan Gunderland. The Dusty Diamond foreman.

"Sorry, ma'am, I didn't mean to spook ya," the old cowboy said, removing his hat with Texas-bred courtesy as he entered the stables.

"That's okay. I'm just a bit jumpy." Recovering her composure, Ally picked up the pitchfork and set it against the wall. "I suppose you're here about the mares?"

"Actually, ma'am, no." He ran his hat brim through his gnarled fingers, making it go round. "I tried to get ya on the phone, but couldn't get through. I'm sorry to tell ya but I'm here with bad news…."

Ally met his sad brown eyes and time slowed. Troy…?

"Raymond Sanderson died last night in Dallas, and Missy Sanderson—" Stan blurred Misty's name and title as he always did "—flew home this morning. She's there all alone."

Time steadied again. Ally released the breath she'd been holding and lowered the hand she'd unconsciously lifted to her throat. "Oh, poor Misty. I'll come right away."

"Thank you, ma'am." Stan looked relieved. "We weren't sure who to call, and Betts—" his wife and the Sanderson house-keeper "—sent me to come get you. Said Missy would need her friends 'round."

"Betts is right. Can I ride over with you?" she asked, suddenly remembering she didn't have a vehicle. "Can you wait while I clean up?"

"Sure."

Stan followed her up to the house, electing to wait on the porch while Ally hurried inside. She quickly cleaned up and changed her clothes, then retrieved her forgotten phone from the pocket of her other jeans. She checked her messages—just Stan's—then dialed Troy's number. When he didn't pick up, she left him a message about Misty's dad, and that she was going to be with Misty, then quickly dialed Kyle's number.

Her brother picked up on the second ring, his voice filled with jubilation. "Hey, sis! You called just in time to congratulate me. I took the first go-round. Eighty-two points!"

"That's great, Kyle—but is Troy there? I've been trying to get hold of him, but he's not answering his phone."

"Nah, he took off."

"Took off?" Ally repeated in confusion. "What do you mean? Was he hurt?"

"Nah, he didn't even ride. He just took off in a big hurry— said he had to get home."

"Oh. Okay," Ally said rather blankly. "Well, if he comes back will you tell him Misty's dad died? And that I went over there?"

"Ah, that's tough. Poor Misty," Kyle said, his deep voice rough with sympathy. "Yeah, sure I will if I see him. Give Misty my best."

"I will," Ally promised, and hung up. She stared at her phone a minute, puzzled. Why would Troy leave the rodeo? Was his knee hurting? Or…her heart sank a little as a more likely answer occurred…maybe he'd heard the news about Raymond Sanderson, and he'd left to be with Misty. Was already there.

When Ally arrived with Stan at Misty's house, however, the

wide driveway that curved up to the modern, contemporary ranch house was empty. Troy's truck was nowhere in sight.

Betts met them at the door. "Misty is in the sunroom," she said, taking the casserole Ally had thought to bring with a brief smile of thanks. Her eyes remained worried as she said, "I'm glad you're here. People need their friends at a time like this."

"No one else is here?" Ally asked as she stepped into the entrance hall.

Betts shook her gray head. "No. Her aunt Ginny is flying in from Missouri. Stan will need to pick her up in a couple of hours—" she glanced at her watch "—but not everyone has heard the news yet, and I want to get a head start in the kitchen before they all arrive."

"Do you want help with the food?"

"No, no, dear—I've got it all covered. You go visit with Misty—help cheer her up. I know she'll feel better after talking with you."

Ally wasn't so sure. She never seemed to know exactly what to say to people in times of grief. Trepidation dogged her as she followed Betts through the ranch house and, in response to the older woman's whispered "Go ahead on in," walked into the solarium designed to showcase a vista of the Dusty Diamond's extensive stables and paddocks, and the green, tree-studded hills beyond.

Misty was sitting in an armchair looking out the big windows. After Betts and Stan's concern, Ally half expected her to be dissolved in tears. Misty turned her head as Ally entered, and although her eyelids were swollen, her husky voice was calm as she said in faint surprise, "Ally! How nice of you to come."

Misty stood up, her brown eyes looking so lost as she determinedly smiled a greeting, that—although Ally wasn't a hugger—she had no trouble at all crossing the room to give her a hug. "I'm sorry, Misty," she said.

Then they both sat, and Misty talked while Ally just listened.

Misty told her about the last few days, and how she'd been with her father at the end. How she'd told him about the baby, how much she wanted it, and how happy he'd been for her. "I should have told him right away," Misty said sadly. "But pregnancy can really mess with your thinking. Now, with him gone, everything just seems, kind of unreal. If you know what I mean?"

Ally did, and she nodded.

Misty lapsed into silence, gazing out the windows again as she gathered her thoughts. Then she looked at Ally. "Is Troy coming?"

"He was at the rodeo when Stan came to get me. But I left him a message on his phone, so I expect he'll come as soon as he gets it."

Misty nodded, as if there could be no doubt, and, despite her sincere sympathy and friendship with the other woman, Ally felt a prick of resentment that the little blonde could be so certain how Troy—how Ally's *husband*—would react.

Maybe her resentment showed, because Misty studied her a moment, then said gently, "He's my brother, you know."

"What!" Ally gripped the arms of her chair, so stunned she would have fallen over if she hadn't been sitting.

"Troy's my brother," Misty repeated. "I thought he might have told you—"

"He didn't."

"No, I can see that." Misty's faint smile disappeared as she added, "And I should have known he wouldn't. You see—" she glanced down, carefully pleating the hem of the white blouse she was wearing "—Troy and I are the only ones who know. He's known for a long time—since he was about sixteen or so. His mother told him."

"But you haven't known as long?"

Misty shook her head. "No, I just found out about a year ago. Your brother and I had a fight over something stupid, and I was upset and I ran into Troy when I was out riding. We got into this deep discussion and, well, he ended up telling me."

She made a sad little grimace. "I'm afraid I didn't take it well. I was upset. With my mom, for cheating on my dad, with Troy's father—" another grimace "—my biological father, even with poor Troy. He wanted to tell Mick, but I made him swear not to tell anyone else and I didn't, either. I was ashamed of my mother for doing what she'd done, but more than that, I didn't want my dad—my *real* dad, because no matter what anyone says, Raymond Sanderson was my real father—to find out. He was so proud of me. He loved me, and I didn't want him hurt."

Ally remained silent, trying to take it all in. So she'd been right, and so wrong. Troy did love Misty—but as a sister.

It explained so much….

Images spiraled through her mind, memories of things he'd said. She felt dizzy. And sick. She could actually feel the blood drain from her face. Cold sweat broke out on her forehead, and she put her head down on her knees, breathing deeply.

As if from a distance, she could hear Misty saying anxiously, "Ally! Are you all right?" but for a minute or so Ally could only nod, she was trying so hard not to faint or throw up.

Slowly, her nausea subsided. She stayed still, waiting for her weak trembling to ease, for her stomach to settle. Finally, she lifted her head.

She looked at Misty, hovering anxiously, and gave her a reassuring smile. "I'm sorry. I must have a touch of the flu. It hits—but then I'm fine. No big deal, really. I didn't mean to alarm you."

By the time Ally finished her explanation, Misty no longer looked alarmed, merely thoughtful. "This flu," she said slowly, "it comes and goes?"

Ally nodded, still a little weak.

"And do you start to perspire, and feel dizzy and shaky, and your throat kind of closes up, while drool just keeps pooling and pooling in your mouth, making you just want to vomit and vomit—"

"Oh, please…" Ally moaned, covering her mouth and swallowing convulsively. "Please, stop. Yes—yes, I feel all of that. But please don't talk about it anymore."

"I won't. But, Ally, I don't think you have the flu. Because that's exactly how I feel at least once, and sometimes twice, a day."

"You do?" Ally looked at her in surprise.

"Yeah."

"So what do you think is causing…" Ally's eyes widened. She pressed her hand against her churning stomach, staring at Misty in disbelief.

Misty nodded. "I think pregnancy is causing it. For both us."

"But I—Troy—" Ally took a deep breath. "We were careful. Except maybe once…"

"Yeah, been there, done that," Misty said with a slight smile and sigh, "and now I'm a poster girl for did-it-only-one-time conception success. Not that I'm sorry," she said with a touch of her usual fierceness, pressing her hand against her own stomach. "I'm thankful to have this baby. And I'm sure, once you get used to the idea—but let's not jump the gun here," she added hastily as Ally moaned again, "until we're completely sure you even are pregnant."

She paused, giving Ally an inquiring look. "I still have the backup to the backup pregnancy test. Do you want to use it?"

"Yes. I think I'd better," Ally said. But she just sat there a moment with her hand against her abdomen, her womb. Because even without taking the test, Ally was one hundred percent certain what it would reveal.

She was going to have a baby.

Troy's baby.

* * *

When Troy got home, Ally wasn't there. He searched the house, anxious to find her, to discover if what Linc had implied could be true—that she cared about him. He flipped on the intercom to the stables and called her name. When he didn't get an answer, he walked down to count horses, making sure she hadn't gone off for a ride by herself and found trouble.

But the horses were all there, and she wasn't at the hammock or working in the barn. She hadn't left him a note anywhere, and Troy was starting to worry when he picked up the phone he'd left on his nightstand to call her, and realized she'd left him a message.

He listened to the news about Raymond Sanderson's death, then immediately tried to call her back. When Ally's voice mail came on, he hung up to call the Dusty Diamond ranch instead.

"Ally just left," Betts told him. "She convinced Misty to lie down awhile—the poor little thing is worn-out with all she's been through—and Ally decided to catch a ride back to Bride's Price with Stan, since he had to drive out to the airport, anyway. She said she'd probably be coming back with you later."

Troy's frown cleared. It sounded as if Ally wasn't angry at him anymore. He asked Betts, "How's Misty holding up?"

"She's doing fine. Just tired."

"Well, tell her I called and I'll see her this evening."

"I will."

Betts hung up and so did Troy, then he glanced at the time. The way he figured it, Ally should be home soon.

As he looked out for her, he saw a big silver truck pulling up the long drive. His grandfather's truck.

Mick parked in front of the house.

"Hey, Mick!" Troy greeted him. "What're you doing here?"

"Thought it was past time I came to see what you've done with the place," Mick said, slapping Troy on the shoulder as he reached him. "How 'bout a tour?"

"Sounds like a plan."

At first, Troy enjoyed showing the old man what he'd accomplished. Mick appreciated all the changes, approved heartily of the rebuilt stables and paddocks. But every time Mick made a comment about how they could "cut back a few trees, put in a pool for the guests" or expand the house "—hell, knock down the whole thing and put in a real hunting lodge—" Troy's enjoyment ebbed a little.

Ally loved that house. She'd worked hard on it.

"We're not going to knock down the house," Troy said shortly.

Mick slanted him a sidelong glance, then slapped him on the back. "We'll talk," he said indulgently. "Plenty of time to make a decision on that. Right now, I could use a beer."

So they headed to the house. Troy took off his hat and grabbed a couple of longnecks. He gave one to his grandfather and they settled in the front room.

"Yeah, you've done a fine job with the place," Mick said, crossing one big booted foot over the other, and resting his bottle on his broad chest.

"Come by later this week," Troy told him, "and we can ride out and I'll show you how that herd I've been working on is coming along."

Mick shook his head in disgust. "Don't know why you're interested in developing your own breed. Our Angus have been here before I came to this county, and they'll be here when we're both long gone."

"But there's always room for improvement," Troy said, repeating what he'd said to the old man a million times before.

On cue, Mick came back with "Fine, but you don't have the time to fool around with the cattle. You need to start getting focused...."

His grandfather was off and running, telling Troy he could start small, run for the Tangleweed city council, maybe. "The people of this town had damn well better vote for you, or they'll answer to me…."

Troy listened with half an ear, imagining Mick rounding up Tangleweed citizens at gunpoint to vote for him, while keeping his other ear cocked for the sound of Stan's truck and Ally's return. Damn, what was taking her so long? He wanted to see her, find out if she cared about him, as Linc had implied.

"We could start up one of those grass roots campaign for you. I have plenty of money set aside to light a fire under that…."

Did he hear an engine? Troy glanced past Mick out the window, craning his neck to see if someone pulled in next to Mick's silver truck. Nope. Nada. No one, damn it.

"We've wasted enough time. We need to get started…."

Where was Ally? She should have been home by now.

Ally made a rueful face to herself when she saw the big silver truck parked in front of the house up ahead.

"Looks like Mick's here," Stan observed next to her as they drove past the stables, obviously having recognized the vehicle, too.

"Umm-hmm." Making a quick decision, Ally said, "Stop here, please, Stan. I need to check something in the stables before I go in."

"Sure thing, Miz O'Malley."

Ally was still smiling as the old cowboy pulled away. *Miz O'Malley*—just like Troy had predicted.

She headed down the path for a brief visit with Boomer, wanting time alone to savor the realization that she was going to have a baby, before she had to go be polite to Mick. Whenever she'd run into him through the years, the old man had always stared right through her. Even at the wedding he'd barely spoken to her, and she wondered if maybe it was because she resembled Eileen when she'd been young.

She shrugged the thought off. Oh, well, it didn't matter. Now that he was going to be her baby's great-grandfather, she'd just have to find a way to get along with the old man—and Troy would have to find a way to get along with her brothers.

She smiled again, thinking of how excited Troy would be when she told him the big news. He'd probably want to send an announcement to the *Tangleweed Times* immediately.

If Ally didn't get home soon—or at least call—he was going to go out and look for her, Troy decided.

"...so I thought we'd invite the senator and his aides here for a hunting party next month."

"Whoa!" That caught Troy's attention. "What are you talking about?"

Mick looked at him impatiently. "I'm saying we'll invite them here, to Bride's Price. Haven't you been listening to me, boy?"

No. "I'm not going to invite anyone here."

"Why not?"

"Ally wouldn't like it." Hell, *he* wouldn't like it. A bunch of strangers—politicians!—marching around the house. Was Mick crazy? Where would they sleep? In the attic? 'Cause he and Ally sure weren't giving up the pink bedroom.

He told Mick, "Put that idea right out of your head."

The sound of Troy's voice stopped Ally in her tracks just as she stepped out of the bright sunlight and into the cool shadows of the straw scented stable. For a moment, she thought Troy was nearby and her smile brightened. Then she heard Mick's voice and realized the intercom to the house was on.

"Why? Who gives a damn if she likes it or not? What could she do?"

"Divorce me."

"Ha! Let her. That's just what we want. Boy, you've pulled off the trick I've been trying for over sixty years. With all the time, labor and money you've put into this ranch, our lawyer will have no problem showing you have a claim on the place. Hell!"

Ally heard Mick chuckle.

"When I heard you'd even invested in stock—picking up those mares Sanderson had to sell off—I thought 'that boy is brilliant.' But like I told you at the wedding, you need to get in and get out. 'Course, that baby you planted in her belly could be a problem...."

"There is no baby."

Troy sounded clipped.

"Good! That makes it perfect, then. All I can say, boy, is that I'm damn proud of you."

Ally stumbled out of the stables, her stomach churning, unable to bear to hear another word. Oh, God, what a fool she'd been. While she'd secretly believed she and Troy were building a relationship, he'd simply been using the idea she'd come up with— her business proposition of a marriage—to stake a legal claim to Bride's Price.

She looked around at the little ranch tucked among the hills. At the whispering trees, the hot, bright sunlight shining down on the pretty little house, the big ancient barn, and the now-sturdy stables.

So, Troy wanted Bride's Price, did he?

She started up the path to the house.

Inside, Troy stared at his grandfather, marveling at how delusional the old man could be.

"Has it ever occurred to you," Troy asked him, "that if we

divorce, Ally will have as much right to claim half the Running M as I would Bride's Price?"

"No, she won't. The Running M is still in my name. Yeah, yeah, I know I told you I was putting your name on the title, but after talking it over with my lawyer, I decided to wait."

Of course he had, Troy thought. Talk about delusional—he was worse than Mick. Had he really expected Mick to give up any amount of power? Give up the one thing he knew Troy craved, the carrot he'd used to get Troy to do what he wanted?

"No need to look at me like that, son. I aim to keep my word—management of the Running M in exchange for Bride's Price. I promise you'll have that deed by the end of the week."

Troy studied his grandfather's hard face in silence. Maybe Mick would finally keep his word. Maybe not. Either way, Troy realized, it really didn't matter. Because he was no longer willing to make that deal.

"Don't bother, Mick. You're not getting Bride's Price."

"What!" Mick straightened in his chair, green eyes glaring. "The hell you say!"

"Yeah, I do say. I don't want Ally to divorce me. I want her to stay married to me for the rest of our lives. My wife is the kindest, the sweetest—"

The door banged open. Ally stamped inside. Without sparing Mick so much as a glance, she glared across the room at Troy.

"So!" she said fiercely, blue eyes blazing, hands on hips, "all along, the reason you went along with my proposition, jumped to get involved in it—involved with *me*—wasn't because you wanted that lease, or thought I might be pregnant, or even to help me out. All you were after was Bride's Price. Well, send me a bill of sale, and I'll sign it—this ranch is yours."

She spun around, then spun back. "Oh, and I almost forgot." Ripping off her ring, she flung it on the floor. "You can take this, too. Unlike my great-aunt, I'm not going to pine away, yearning after something that never existed in the first place. I'm getting out of this place, out of Tangleweed and, most of all, I'm getting away from you!"

She reached for the door handle—then turned back once again to grab his keys. "And I'm taking your truck!"

The door slammed behind her.

"Huh?" For a dumbfounded second, Troy didn't move. Then he leaped to his feet. "Ally! Ally, wait!"

He started for the door, but his grandfather got in his way, tripping him up.

"Move, Mick!"

Mick stubbornly stood still. "Don't be a fool, son. Don't you see? You've done it! You've gotten back Bride's Price. "

Tires squealed.

"Damn it, Mick—" Troy reached the porch just in time to see his black truck fly down the drive like a bat out of hell.

Troy stared after it cursing, then strode back into the house. Mick was planted in the middle of the room. "Don't take it hard, son. No woman's worth worrying over, believe me."

Troy ignored him, scanning the floor, searching behind the chair.

Mick's iron-gray brows lowered in a frown. "What are you doing?"

"I'm looking for her ring."

"Why?"

Right then Troy saw it, glinting next to the end table. He scooped it up, dropped it in his pocket.

He picked up his hat and slipped it on, then turned to his grandfather. "Keep the Running M. You want control, you can have it. But Bride's Price is Ally's and Ally's mine and it's going to remain that way."

He started toward the door, and Mick's hand shot out, strong bony fingers locking on his forearm.

Mick's eyes narrowed to vicious green slits. "If you go chasing after that little Cabrerra bitch, you're dead to me—do you hear me, boy? *Dead.*"

For a long moment, Troy studied his grandfather's face, the green eyes, the square jaw so like his own. Then, "I can live with that," he said quietly.

Breaking the old man's hold without effort, Troy left.

Chapter Thirteen

"Finally, never evaluate the results of your breeding program based on just one season. Time is always necessary to determine failure or success. In the future, even a seeming mistake may lead to a remarkable outcome."
      —*Successful Breeding: A Guide for the Cattleman*

Ally pulled up in front of the Circle C in a flurry of dust. No sooner had she shut off the powerful engine, than Cole strode out the door to greet her.

For once, a smile lit up his hard face. "Ally! I was just going to call you!" His deep voice was filled with excitement. "We did it, Al! We did it! Vorquez has found oil."

"That's good," Ally said, walking up to the porch.

She would have walked right past him, but Cole caught her arm, gently pulling her to a halt.

"Wait a minute. What's wrong?" he asked, his smile fading as he studied her face. "Are you all right?"

Ally swallowed as the concern in his deep voice threatened her control on the tears she'd been fighting.

"Ally!" Cole sounded shaken. "You *never* cry."

"I'm not crying," Ally insisted, her voice husky as she swiped at her wet eyes with her palm. "I'm just—angry. And upset. And pregnant."

"Pregnant!" Cole's grip on her arm tightened. "But Luke told us you swore you weren't pregnant when you got married."

"I wasn't. Then. But I am now. And—oh, I just hate that Troy O'Malley."

"Why? What—?"

The roar of an engine hurtling toward the house interrupted his question, and Cole frowned at the sight of a familiar silver truck. "What's old Mick doing here?" he growled.

But it wasn't Mick, it was Troy who sprang out almost before the huge tires quit spinning.

His gaze shot straight to Ally. "Ally, we need to talk," he said in a determined tone, slamming the door and striding toward her.

"She doesn't want to talk to you, O'Malley." Cole stepped off the porch to intercept the other man. "Not after what you've done."

Troy ignored him, his gaze fixed on Ally. "You've got it all wrong—"

"No, she doesn't."

"I'm not trying to take Bride's Price from you," Troy insisted.

Ally's chin lifted. "That's not what I heard when you were talking to Mick!"

"You heard wrong, then. I'd never take the ranch away from you."

"Sure you wouldn't," Cole scoffed.

Troy's gaze refused to waver from her face. "I love you, Ally."

Ally's heart seemed to stop.

Troy's tone turned coaxing, pleading. "Come home with me, sweetheart. So we can talk this all out."

The sincerity in his voice—on his face—made Ally's heart pound. But before she could reply, Cole spoke up. "She's not going anywhere, not with you," he said, his voice harsh and angry.

Suddenly, Troy turned on him. "Stay out of this," he warned, his green eyes narrowing menacingly. "This is between me and my wife."

"She won't be your wife for long. She's divorcing your sorry ass." Hunching his broad shoulders, Cole lifted his fists threateningly. "Now, get off our land."

Troy's hands fisted, too. "Make me," he snarled.

Ally blinked. *Make me?* What were they? Ten?

Apparently so, because both men lunged and fists and hats and dust started flying. Boots slid and scuffled on the dirt. Curses and grunts filled the air.

"Oh, for goodness' sake… Stop it!" Ally demanded. "Both of you!"

They kept swinging, breathing heavily, still cursing. Troy jabbed shrewdly, and Cole reared back, his lip bleeding. Cole swung viciously, grazing Troy's cheek.

"Stop it right now!"

Cole swung again, catching Troy in the stomach. Troy bent with a grunt, then rallied with a hard punch to Cole's ribs.

"Damn it!" Ally fought the urge to rush between them. If they hurt the baby… "You're getting me upset," she yelled at them.

They ignored her.

Ally put her hands on her hips. "*Troy Michael O'Malley.* Do you want to hurt our *baby?*"

Troy stopped in midswing, his head swiveling in her direction. "Baby?"

"Yeah, you bastard. She's having a baby and you're getting her upset." Cole's fist landed on Troy's jaw, knocking him off his feet. Panting heavily, Cole stood over Troy, grim satisfaction emanating from his tall figure. "That's for getting my sister pregnant," he growled.

"Cole!" Ally rushed over and pushed him aside. "You hurt him!" She crouched next to Troy, cradling his head in her arms. "Oh, Troy... Are you all right?"

He stared up at her, his head resting on her breasts, a dazed look on his face. "I'm fine, but— Did you mean it?"

She nodded, biting her lip.

"Well, then— Hell! Let me get up!"

Ally helped Troy to stand, and once on his feet, he grasped her elbows, holding her still to study her eyes. "So we're having a baby? For real this time?"

She nodded again. "For real this time."

Slowly Troy smiled. Ally slowly smiled back. He lowered his head, while she went up on tiptoe to meet his lips. He kissed her and Ally sighed with pleasure as her surroundings began to dim—

"Ah, damn it, Ally. Make up your mind," Cole said in exasperation. "I thought you hated the guy."

Reluctantly, Ally broke the kiss to regard her brother apologetically. "I'm sorry, Cole. I shouldn't have put you in the middle. I overheard Mick and Troy talking—"

Troy's hold tightened around her waist.

"—and I got upset. All I could think of was escaping to the Circle C, which wasn't fair to you. Misty's right," Ally added, suddenly remembering what her friend had told her, "being pregnant can really mess with your thinking."

"Misty?" Cole frowned, fastening on the name. "What does Misty have to do with any of this?"

"Well," drawled Troy, "since she's pregnant, too—"

"Misty's pregnant!" Cole stared at him in frozen surprise.

"Yeah," Troy set Ally gently aside and took a step toward her brother. "That's right, Misty is pregnant—with *your* baby." His fist shot out, hitting Cole's jaw and sending him sprawling.

"Troy!" Ally clutched at his arm.

But Troy was finished. He rubbed his sore knuckles with grim satisfaction as he stared at the man stretched out in the dirt. "That's for getting *my* sister pregnant."

"Your sister!" Cole exclaimed, sitting upright.

Troy nodded.

"Misty's his half sister," Ally explained. "Troy's father was running off with Misty's mother the night they were killed."

Cole staggered to his feet, a bewildered expression on his hard face. "How do you know all this?"

"Misty told me. And she also told us—Troy and me, that is— that she's pregnant with your baby. About seven or eight weeks, I think. Is that about right?"

Ally glanced at Troy for confirmation—and caught him wincing as he gingerly fingered his square jaw.

"What's wrong?" Ally demanded, forgetting about Misty. "Is your jaw broken?"

"Not sure." Troy opened and closed his mouth, but flinched away when Ally reached up to feel along his cheek for herself. "Hey—"

She traced his jawline with careful fingertips, scolding, "Don't be such a baby."

"Baby!"

"Yes. You ride bulls for a living, get bucked off constantly, but one little punch—"

"I don't get bucked off *constantly*," Troy corrected her indignantly. "At least half the time I jump off. Or," he amended, "I used to."

"Used to?" She rested her hand gently against his cheek as she looked at him questioningly.

"Yeah, I've decided to quit bull riding." He looked down at her, watched her eyes grow so big and joyful that he had to press a kiss against her slim wrist, so near to his mouth.

"Oh, Troy…"

Her pulse beat against his lips. He kissed her wrist again, then narrowed his eyes at her as he added, "And I'm not being a baby. I'll have you know your brother packs a hell of a wallop. Don't you, you son of—" Troy turned to berate Cole and found he'd disappeared. "Hey! Where'd he go?"

An engine cranking to life answered him, and Troy glared at the battered blue truck backing out. "Well, would you look at that. He's taking off—and without his hat, too!" he added, catching sight of it still lying in the dirt.

He picked up his own hat, knocked the dirt off the charcoal felt, re-creased it and set it on his head. Tilting the brim down, he slanted a glance at Ally. "I must have scared him pretty bad," he concluded smugly.

"Oh, stop." She gave his hard shoulder an absent shove. "He's going to see Misty, and you know it. Cole!" Ally waved, trying to get her brother's attention. "Cole! Wait!"

But he ignored her, gunning the motor as he headed down the road.

"I hope he's okay to drive after being knocked down like that." Ally spared Troy a reproving glance. "I forgot to tell him about Misty's dad."

Troy put his arm around her shoulders. "He'll find out when he gets there."

"Still, if he'd bothered to wait, I could have warned him—but, no, he couldn't stop to listen. He never listens to me." Her gaze narrowed on the retreating truck. "None of them do."

"I do," Troy declared, dragging her into his arms, wanting her attention on *him*—where it belonged—and not her bullheaded brothers. "I listen to every word you say."

She gave him such a skeptical look that Troy had to repress a smile. But he kept his voice stern. "Right now, however, I want you listen to me." He tilted her chin up to meet her eyes. "I don't know exactly what you overheard, but if I ever thought I could take Bride's Price from you, I was just fooling myself."

She hesitated. "But Mick said—"

"He was wrong. Besides which…well, I don't think we'll be seeing much of Mick in the future. He disowned me."

"Oh, I'm sure he didn't mean it." Ally smoothed his hair back from the scrape on his temple. She didn't like Mick, but he was Troy's grandfather. "He can't be that angry if he lent you his car to come after me."

Troy grinned wryly. "Actually," he drawled, "I stole it. Then I had to call the Running M on the way here to tell the foreman to pick Mick up at Bride's Price."

"Oh, Troy. You took his truck?"

"Wasn't anything else I could do, since you stole mine running away from me." He gave her a reproving squeeze."

"I'll never do that again," she promised solemnly. "Next time we argue, I'll stay right there so you can *listen* to me. Over and over and over again."

He winced, and she smiled, then gave him a hug. "Maybe Mick will come around," she whispered to comfort him.

"Yeah, well, I realized today he's never going to change, and neither am I. He's got dreams of me taking up where he left off. Going into politics. All my dreams are tied up with you." His voice deepened, grew huskier, as he added, "I love you, Ally. I want you to have everything in life that you want. Do you love me?"

Her blue gaze softened. "You know I do." She reached up to stroke his bruised cheek gently. "I love you with all my heart."

The words, the feel of her small hand on his whisker-rough skin, felt so good, so *right*, that a surge of aching happiness fisted in Troy's gut.

His arms tightened. "Okay, so no more talk about divorce or temporary marriages. You're mine forever. Speaking of which—"

He fished in his pocket and drew out the little circlet of diamonds. Lifting her hand, he slipped the ring on her finger and gave it an admonitory tap. "Don't you ever take this off again. This is an *eternity* ring."

"It is?"

"Yeah. That's what it means when the diamonds go all the way round on a band like that."

"It does?" Ally regarded him curiously. "How do you know something like that?"

"Because that's what the clerk at Tiffany's told me."

"Tiffany's!" Her blue eyes rounded. "Oh, Troy, Tiffany's is so *expensive*."

He lifted a brow. "You want me to take it back?"

"Not on your life!"

Her fierce expression made him chuckle—which made him have to kiss her again. And she kissed him back so well that he finally had to stop to swing her up into his arms, so she could wrap her arms tightly around his neck, just the way he liked it.

He rubbed his cheek on her silky hair. "I love you, Ally O'Malley. Let's go home and celebrate our new baby."

"Let's!" she agreed.

And they headed home to Bride's Price.

* * * * *

EXPECTING ROYAL TWINS! *by Melissa McClone*

Mechanic Izzy was shocked when a tall handsome prince strode into her workshop and declared he was her husband! Now she's about to face an even bigger surprise...

TO DANCE WITH A PRINCE *by Cara Colter*

Royal playboy Kiernan's been nicknamed Prince Heartbreaker. Meredith knows, in her head, that he's the last man she needs, yet her heart thinks otherwise!

HONEYMOON WITH THE RANCHER *by Donna Alward*

After Tomas' fiancée's death, he sought peace on his Argentine ranch. Until socialite Sophia arrived for her honeymoon...*alone*. Can they heal each other's hearts?

NANNY NEXT DOOR *by Michelle Celmer*

Sydney's ex left her with nothing, but she needs to provide for her daughter. Sheriff Daniel's her new neighbour who could give Sydney the perfect opportunity.

A BRIDE FOR JERICHO BRAVO *by Christine Rimmer*

After being jilted by her long-time boyfriend, Marnie's given up on love. Until meeting sexy rebel Jericho has her believing in second chances...

Cherish

Her Not-So-Secret Diary
by Anne Oliver

Sophie's fantasies stayed secret—until her saucy dream was accidentally e-mailed to her sexy boss! But as their steamy nights reach boiling point, Sophie knows she's in a whole heap of trouble...

The Wedding Date
by Ally Blake

Under no circumstances should Hannah's gorgeous boss, Bradley, be considered her wedding date! Now, if only her disobedient legs would do the *sensible* thing and walk away...

Molly Cooper's Dream Date
by Barbara Hannay

House-swapping with London-based Patrick has given Molly the chance to find a perfect English gentleman! Yet she's increasingly curious about Patrick himself—is the Englishman she wants on the other side of the world?

If the Red Slipper Fits...
by Shirley Jump

It's not *unknown* for Caleb Lewis to find a sexy stiletto in his convertible, but Caleb usually has some recollection of how it got there! He's intrigued to meet the woman it belongs to...

On sale from 4th March 2011
Don't miss out!

Available at WHSmith, Tesco, ASDA, Eason and all good bookshops

www.millsandboon.co.uk

Nora Roberts' *The O'Hurleys*

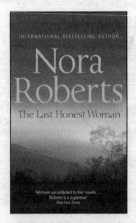

4th March 2011

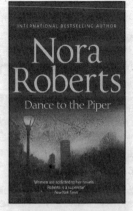

1st April 2011

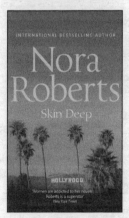

6th May 2011

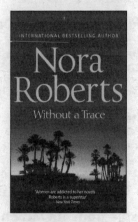

3rd June 2011

www.millsandboon.co.uk

2 FREE BOOKS
AND A SURPRISE GIFT

We would like to take this opportunity to thank you for reading this Mills & Boon® book by offering you the chance to take TWO more specially selected books from the Cherish™ series absolutely FREE! We're also making this offer to introduce you to the benefits of the Mills & Boon® Book Club™—

- **FREE home delivery**
- **FREE gifts and competitions**
- **FREE monthly Newsletter**
- **Exclusive Mills & Boon Book Club offers**
- **Books available before they're in the shops**

Accepting these FREE books and gift places you under no obligation to buy, you may cancel at any time, even after receiving your free books. Simply complete your details below and return the entire page to the address below. You don't even need a stamp!

YES Please send me 2 free Cherish books and a surprise gift. I understand that unless you hear from me, I will receive 5 superb new stories every month, including two 2-in-1 books priced at £5.30 each, and a single book priced at £3.30, postage and packing free. I am under no obligation to purchase any books and may cancel my subscription at any time. The free books and gift will be mine to keep in any case.

Ms/Mrs/Miss/Mr _____ Initials _____

Surname _____
Address _____

_____ Postcode _____
E-mail _____

Send this whole page to: Mills & Boon Book Club, Free Book Offer, FREEPOST NAT 10298, Richmond, TW9 1BR